Bushwa

Lockwood
The Accidental Sheriff
Beware a Pale Horse
Trouble

Sioux Sunrise
Paint the Hills Red
Grit
Cut Nose
The Long Walk
Coldsmith
Ghost of the Guadalupe

Bushwa

Ron Schwab

Uplands Press
OMAHA, NEBRASKA

Uplands Press
1401 S 64th Avenue
Omaha, NE 68106
www.uplandspress.com

Publisher's Note: This is a work of fiction. Names, characters, places, and incidents are a product of the author's imagination. Locales and public names are sometimes used for atmospheric purposes. Any resemblance to actual people, living or dead, or to businesses, companies, events, institutions, or locales is completely coincidental.

Ordering Information:
Quantity sales. Special discounts are available on quantity purchases by corporations, associations, and others. For details, contact the "Special Sales Department" at the address above.

Uplands Press / Ron Schwab -- 1st ed.
ISBN 978-1-943421-70-1

Chapter 1

February 1862

OBADIAH SPARKS SAT on the east bank of the Rio Grande River, his sore, bare feet dangling in the water. He was Obadiah only to his mother, if she still lived, which he doubted. It had been a good five years since he visited her back in South Carolina, and she had been on the edge of death then. Everybody else knew him as "Bushwa" Sparks, and that was how he signed his name. That was as far as his writing went.

As a boy growing up in rural South Carolina, some taunting boy had called him "Bushwa" after he told one of his lies, and once Bushwa had beaten the boy's face to apple pulp, he decided he liked the sound of the moniker and adopted it as his name. Only later did he learn that the French had first brought the term to America via the phrase *bois de vache* or "wood of the cow" in reference to cow droppings or buffalo dung, which were an essential source of fire fuel in vast treeless areas.

It did not take long for westerners to further Anglicize the term to "bullshit." Bushwa's legendary storytelling somehow made the name a logical fit. It did not matter a whit to Bushwa. He carried the name with pride. He had always hated Obadiah.

The depressing odor of blood and death lingered out here in the middle of New Mexico Territory where the fighting had ended almost two days earlier. An occasional corpse or bodiless arm or head still floated down the river that split the territory north and south and would eventually become much of the border between Mexico and the United States. He guessed the Confederate States of America might supplant the latter, depending upon the outcome of this fool war, but he doubted it.

The Confederate Brigadier General, Henry H. Sibley, was declaring victory because of the withdrawal of Union troops by Colonel Edward Canby from the battlefield at Valverde. Sibley had spent the two-day battle in an ambulance wagon claiming to be sick but was more likely drunk, Bushwa figured. Colonel Thomas Green had assumed command and not embarrassed himself anyhow, it appeared.

The Confederate forces had been unable to overpower the stone-walled Fort Craig some six miles to the south, and there was talk now that Sibley was planning to head north to Albuquerque and then on to Santa Fe. Bushwa hoped they had a pleasant journey, because he was not going with them. He was a volunteer with the Fourth Texas Cavalry Regiment, which had yesterday evening, because of devastating loss of horses, been declared an infantry regiment. Bushwa Sparks had no intention of walking all the way to Santa Fe, or even ten miles upriver for that matter.

"Bushwa, I've been looking all over for you. What are you doing down here by the river?"

He did not even turn to identify the speaker. Winston Evans, barely twenty years old, had worked for him in Jefferson, Texas, joined the volunteers with him, and tagged along from the east end of Texas to the west side and north into this barren land. Win, a corporal now, outranked Bushwa, who had been top sergeant twice and drunk and fought his way down to private, where he was now. With the number of men who died or were badly wounded at Valverde, there would be some rank shifting again. Maybe he would stay on if they would make him a captain and give him a horse. It did not matter much. They wore no uniforms or insignia, and in this so-called army, few men paid much attention to rank.

"Bushwa, you didn't answer me."

"Well, Corporal, sir, I am soaking my sore feet."

Evans came up and sat down beside him. "After chow this noon, they want the Fourth to line up and take some instructions in infantry formation. It appears they meant it when they said we're done with horses. Any Fourth Cavalry horses will go into the remudas for the other cavalry regiments. It doesn't seem quite right, since a lot of the men own their own horses."

Bushwa said, "Since I lost my gray gelding when we was kicking the Federals out of Fort Stockton, I've been stuck on that dang bay, and he don't like me any better than I do him—bites me when he gets the chance. Still, sitting on that critter beats walking ten thousand miles."

"Not that far."

"Too dang far, whatever it turns out to be. I'll be forty years old next birthday. I ain't walked a half mile the last ten if I had me a horse close by. I won't be going."

They sat there silently for some minutes, two men who seemed an unlikely pair. Bushwa was a black-bearded man wearing a skunk skin cap with the tail dangling over his neck to meld into the long hair hanging there. He was a bearish, barrel-chested man, stout but not flabby or paunchy and stood an inch or two short of six feet.

Win Evans, on the other hand, was lean and sinewy, standing a strong two inches over six feet, light brown hair barely falling to his neck. He had a week's growth of whiskers on his face, but that would be shaved clean at first opportunity. He had finished ten years of school when his father died, leaving him orphaned five years earlier. He was, accordingly, a well-educated man for this time and place.

Win had latched onto Bushwa when seeking work on the docks at Jefferson, Texas. Win, an Iowa farm boy, headed south after his father's death and ended up in the small town that bustled with commerce. Bushwa had owned a small cargo vessel that transported goods and farm produce to and from the Mississippi River less than ten miles distant. Bushwa had been looking to hire two men but recognized a bargain in the strapping youngster and settled for one. Win had carved out a permanent job with the older man, his education making him indispensable to a man without a single year of formal schooling who could do little more than sign his own name and read a simple sentence with serious study.

The two had been a match, though, and for nearly five years they had been like father and son. He was not ready to let go of Bushwa. "You will be shot or hanged if you desert."

"I ain't deserting. I'm retiring. I was a volunteer. Now I am un-volunteering. I didn't sign no papers. Neither of us did. We just went along with some others. My think-box must have been addled. I got no stake in this war. I don't own a slave and never did, never wanted to. I just never liked most Yankees, and the South has always been home. Hell, not one out of ten men in the regiment comes from a slave-holding family. They're just siding with their homeland."

"I don't know what to say. This war never made sense to me—Americans killing each other—but I've been living in the South, and I guess I just followed you."

"Well, kid, I'm leaving tonight, and you've got to decide who you're going to follow before the day's out."

"It bothers me to just pull up stakes and run, but I've got to admit I've been wondering lately what I'm doing here. I was born and raised in Iowa. I am against slavery, and any kin I've got will be wearing blue. I've got at least three cousins up that way that have likely been called to serve. But I don't want to be a coward."

"You ain't a coward, Win. I seen you fighting at Valverde. You didn't give an inch. When your horse went down, you got right back on your feet and faced them devils moving in on you. I was too far away to help, and I feared for your life, but you stood your ground and kilt two before some of our boys showed up and saved your skin. You got grit, Win. You'll do."

"I just don't know if I could live with it. Still, I felt like I was fighting my own people when shooting at the Yankees."

"I won't carry an ounce of guilt when I walk away. I did two years in the Mexican War under General Zachary Taylor, an old Southern boy."

"You knew President Taylor?" Win asked.

"Well, I saw him once. I served under General Winfield Scott along with both Grant and Lee. They was young officers then, and I was the first sergeant for Captain Robert E. Lee for a spell. Later, he got some brevet promotions thanks to my advice. Ulysses Grant and Lee was friends in them days. But it was Scott, Lee, and me that was responsible for the taking of Mexico City. Well, Scott took all the credit, but he couldn't have done it without us."

"I've got to think on this. If I choose to stay, I won't say a word about your taking off, but I guess that makes me sort of a traitor, too."

"Win, you just got too dang much conscience. You think about things too much. Do what your gut says sometimes. Is this your war?"

"Where do we go, if we leave here?"

"I thought I would head south to El Paso. It's this side of the Mexican border, but the Mexican town of Juarez is just across the Rio Grande River if we decide it's best to escape the country till the war's done. The rebellion will be put down by the North sooner or later, and then there won't be any army for us to be in trouble with."

"You don't speak Spanish."

"Nope, I never learnt any Mexican to speak of, but you picked some up from that pretty Mexican gal you was sniffing around in Jefferson for almost a year. That pretty little Valeria. You never told me if you ever got a poke."

"That's not your concern, Bushwa. I've got me some thinking to do."

"Don't think too hard. Let me know by midafternoon. I'll be planning this out—well, not much to plan, really. Just get a horse and go."

Chapter 2

Bushwa's arguments for departing the war became increasingly persuasive as Win Evans thought about his friend's plans, but he remained wary of the storyteller's impulsiveness. The man had a good heart at his core, but he tended to go with his gut instead of his brain, and Win never knew what to believe when words flowed from Bushwa's mouth. Truth could be difficult to sort out when he spoke. Sometimes it seemed that Bushwa had difficulty distinguishing between truth and fiction once he uttered words and that words spoken became his own truth.

Win marched in formation now with others of the former cavalry brigade over dirt and sand of the semi-arid flatlands that had been staked out for a crude parade ground a short distance from their bivouac along the Rio Grande. While he did not look forward to being an infantryman, he decided he could handle it better than most. Many were struggling to maintain the pace, and there was ample grumbling in the ranks.

He noticed that Bushwa had not shown up for drills, but neither had half the regiment. He figured there were no more than two hundred men here, but no roll call had been taken. He could not recall roll call ever being taken and wondered if the army even had a formal roster of the volunteers. They had been divided into five companies, skipping a brigade identification because of a shortage of men and officers. Win and Bushwa had been assigned to Company B. The five companies were separated on the parade ground with an assortment of former cavalry officers trying to create marching units. Win could see that there was little chance these men would be marching as units for any distance. He envisioned ragtag soldiers strung out across the desert.

The second lieutenant in command of Company B called a halt, and without waiting for a command, many of the men dropped to their knees in exhaustion. Staff Sergeant Ferdinand Weisel waved for Win to join him. Win fell out of line and walked over to the sergeant, stopped, came to attention, and saluted when he reached him.

"At ease, Corporal," Sergeant Weisel said. "I just have a few questions."

"Yessir."

Weisel studied him for a moment. He was a short, stocky man with a black mustache and steel-gray eyes that were studying him like a book. "We are missing half the men. What's the scuttlebutt?"

"I don't understand, sir."

"What are the men saying? Are we looking at desertions?"

"I don't know why, sir. But I haven't heard such talk. I don't know if anybody would say anything around me, though."

"But they don't like the notion of being afoot, do they?"

"No, sir, I suppose not, but I don't, either. But I understand that there is not much choice."

"At least you are honest about it. I don't like it, either. I've always been a horse soldier. I had fifteen years in the Union army when war broke out, but I knew where I belonged."

"I understand, sir."

"I wonder if you do. You're not a southerner. Your talk gives you away. Where are you from?"

"I am a Texan, sir, but I was born and raised in Iowa. I came to Texas at fifteen."

"How old are you?"

"Twenty, sir."

"Where is your friend, former Sergeant Sparks?"

"I saw him this morning, sir. His foot was ailing. He wasn't certain he would make it to drills this afternoon."

"Is he likely to desert?"

"Private Sparks? I can't imagine."

"He's a hell of a good man in combat, but there wasn't anybody better than you at Valverde, Corporal. You showed you could lead others and kill when you had to. You could have a future in the army. I hope you and Sparks will stay. I would hate to see you in front of a firing squad or hanging from a tree branch."

"I understand, sir."

"And I would like you to spread the word that deserters will be shot or hanged. That word comes straight from General Sibley."

It was midafternoon when the company was dismissed from the parade ground, and Win decided instantly to seek out Bushwa. They needed to talk.

He figured he would find the ornery cuss somewhere along the river. Bushwa was a natural river rat and hated the desert-like country they were in now. He had complained for days during the trek across West Texas about the lack of water and dried-up creek beds. Win walked along the riverbank, passing a scattering of soldiers along the way who were absorbed with and evidently finding solace there after a few days of war and bloodshed. Finally, he came upon Bushwa who was cocooned in a filthy blanket on the ground in a cluster of small cottonwood trees, sleeping and snoring with soft, hog-like grunt sounds.

Win thought that Bushwa did not look like a man tortured with the agony of serious decision-making. It occurred to him that he had never seen the man fret about choices to be made. Again and again, he had heard his friend and employer declare. "A man has just got to pick the white horse or the black horse. You can use the same saddle." Or he might say, "It don't matter none which fork in the road you take. Both the right and the left trails take you someplace."

Well, Win had been agonizing about his decision, and he preferred to know more about that horse beneath the saddle and where those trails off the fork led. He could not be more different than his mentor, and yet he was somehow bonded with this character.

"Bushwa," Win said. "Wake up. We've got to talk."

Bushwa moaned, and his head emerged from the blankets like a turtle's head from its shell. "What's the matter with you, Win? It's siesta time," he said with his gravelly voice.

"I don't know how you can sleep if you are still thinking about pulling out."

Bushwa sat up and tossed the blanket aside. "Nothing to think about. I'm leaving after sunset."

"Sarge Weisel told me that General Sibley has sent orders that deserters are to be hanged or shot before a firing squad."

"Already figured as much. That's only if they get caught."

"But you don't know if you will be caught or not."

"Odds are heavy on my side. That's all life is anyhow. Riding with or against the odds. I'm riding with the odds this time. We've had men retire all across Texas on this crazy man's journey—I'm guessing over two hundred from all the regiments. Have you seen anybody shot or hanged yet?"

"Well, now that you mention it, I haven't."

"They ain't got the men or experience to chase down everybody that's dropping off, and I'm guessing this new infantry's going to be missing a passel. Some are likely gone. I seen some walk out of here not even leading a horse behind. Damned fools. If you're going to walk, I don't know if it makes more sense to walk north to the

Union troops or south to the Apaches. Given a walking choice, I'm thinking I would just as soon stick around and march north. But I ain't walking."

"So how do you get a horse?"

"Oh, I've got me a dapple-gray gelding all picked out. He is in the remuda now. Belonged to Captain McDougal who got hisself kilt up at Valverde. Good man."

"But the Confederate army claims the horse now."

"They got no more claim than me. I think the good captain would've wanted me to have that horse. I'm thinking I inherited the critter."

"I see." But he did not.

"Well, Win. From the way you're talking, I take it you're staying on with the regiment."

"No. I guess I am going with you. If this is my war, I'm thinking I am fighting on the wrong side. My people all live in the North, and I think the United States ought to stay in one piece. I just wish I could stop this business of brother killing brother. This is a politicians' war, and it ought to be fought in Washington."

"You've been listening some to me, it appears. You got a horse in mind?"

"No. I haven't picked a horse, and you will have to tell me how to get one."

"I'll pick your critter when I go out to the remuda this evening. I intend to tell the head wrangler out there that Sibley wants the dapple-gray and another mount and that I've been ordered to fetch the horses."

"He will believe you?"

"What are the odds?"

"Yeah, I suppose he will."

"I've got tack including two saddles hidden in the brush a mile or so down river. Did that yesterday. Empty saddlebags there."

"You were dang sure I was coming along it appears."

"Odds favored that. You see if you can pilfer some bread or hardtack, maybe some jerky. We will need to find our own food along the way, hunt and fish when we can. Bring your Spencer and pistol and all the ammunition you can muster. I'm bringing my Sharps rifle and Army Colt—and, of course, my banjo. You will want to make off with a few blankets for your bedroll, but it's best we travel light for now. Pack horse would slow us down, and we need to put some distance between us and the army before daylight."

Bushwa was making this sound too easy. "Where do we meet up?"

"Where I've got the saddles. It's at the first west bend in the river from here. You will find a solid stand of creo-

sote bushes set back from the river's edge. They're en-
tangled bad, and you won't see the tack at first, but that
was the idea. If I'm not there first, just stay put. If I don't
show up within an hour after sundown, you had best return to the encampment. It would likely mean that old
Bushwa lost this toss of the dice. I ain't worried none,
though."

Chapter 3

WIN HAD NO difficulty locating the saddles and gear. He noticed that Bushwa already had a bedroll, his Sharps, and a rawhide bag of other items tucked away in the brush—and, of course, the banjo stuffed into a scuffed and tattered leather case. Bushwa had a bulging deerskin pouch of gold coins that he would stuff in the saddlebags, but it was likely hidden separately nearby.

He must have embarked on his mission to retrieve horses. Win worried about this stunt, but he had worried through a lot of Bushwa's schemes, and most generally worked out fine. Most, not all.

He was increasingly nervous as the minutes ticked away. A glance at his pocket watch told him that it was an hour and a half since sundown. Bushwa had told him to return to the encampment when an hour had passed.

Of course, the man never carried a timepiece and did not have the best sense of time passage, especially if he was telling a story. Win decided to wait another half hour.

Half an hour passed, and Win had just started picking up his gear and supplies when he heard a horse whinny upriver. He tensed and waited, and soon Bushwa appeared leading two horses, one apparently the dapple gray he had coveted, although Win could not be certain in the darkness.

"Howdy, Win. I got the critters. Wrangler didn't want to let the dapple gray go, but I told him that Sibley would be madder than hell if I didn't show up with it, and he gave in. I think he had his eyes on that one for hissself. I brung you a tall blood bay gelding—figured he'd match up with them long legs of yours."

There were none better than Bushwa as a judge of good horseflesh, so Win was not the least concerned about the quality of his selected mount. Bushwa unfailingly came out ahead in the horse-trading business, one of his many enterprises back in Jefferson, Texas.

Bushwa got down on his hands and knees and crawled back into the brush, returning soon with the sand-covered bag of coins. After the horses were saddled and the saddlebags were stuffed with cartridges and their meager supplies, they rode away from the river's edge. "We want to keep the river in sight," Bushwa said, "but there will be men afoot close to the river, and a few might be looking to steal some horses even if it meant trying to kill the riders—not that I would hesitate to feed them a few lead slugs first."

"Yeah, that makes sense. Do you still have El Paso in mind as our destination?"

"Might stop at Las Cruces, a day or two north of El Paso and get supplied, pick up a bit of war gossip maybe. It's smaller and got more Anglos that speak American. Might learn something there before we move on. Mesilla's a bigger town and just across the river off the west bank. Feller told me that our Reb friends chased the Yankees out of Mesilla and Fort Fillmore nearby and claim Mesilla these days. Supposed to be some kind of Confederate capital."

Two days later, their pilfered rations were depleted. Bushwa said, "I ain't seen so much as a skinny rabbit out here in this damned desert, but you can see mountain country off to the west across the river. I'm thinking we should find deer or something to fill our bellies over that way. Can't be more than a half day's ride, and we wouldn't be straying that far from the Rio Grande."

Win did not have a better idea but was dubious about the distance. It was midmorning, though, so they should still reach the mountainous country with ample daylight remaining. "Nothing to eat here but yucca and cactuses and plants that are as likely poisonous as they are edible. I have got a lot to learn about this country."

"Well, I ain't been out this way other than with the volunteers, and we come up more from the east, but if a man keeps his eyes open he can learn fast enough."

It was past sundown when they reached the mountain foothills and reined in for the night in a shallow canyon that offered a healthy stream that snaked its way down from the craggy mountain slopes and was lined with patches of grass for grazing by the horses. At least the critters would eat this night.

They made a cold camp even though the nights brought a biting chill in the few weeks before spring. They still had coffee, but Bushwa said, "We could be in Apache country. No sense in sending out invitations."

Those words did nothing to help Win sleep. He decided that night that he was finished letting Bushwa do the thinking for both. This "retirement" had not been carefully plotted, and he had likely been a fool to sign on. But there was no turning back.

Win said, "We should post a watch tonight. I'll take the first three hours. If you will take three, then I will finish up."

"We don't need no watch. We're hid out good in this little canyon. We're safe enough if we don't light us up a fire."

"Well, I'm going to be watching."

"Oh, hell, wake me up when it's my turn. I don't use timepieces, you know. I go by the moon."

Yes, Win thought, and the moon had always disappeared by the time Bushwa awakened. "I will wake you."

Later, when he shook Bushwa awake, his friend was not happy but crawled out of his bedroll and took the spot Win had claimed as a watch-post on a stone outcropping along the canyon wall above their campsite. Win cocooned himself in his own blankets and dropped off to sleep. His internal alarm woke him three hours later even though Bushwa had failed to summon him.

When Win got up, he could hear Bushwa snoring from his perch above the campsite. He stepped nearer and found Bushwa sitting on the outcropping not more than five feet above ground level. Sharps rifle cradled in his lap and back against the canyon wall. His head drooped forward so that his chin rested on his chest.

Win decided to let the man sleep a spell. The horses were staked out downstream near the camp, and, after retrieving his rifle from its scabbard beside his bedroll, he walked downstream to confirm that the mounts were secure. He noticed that the blood bay seemed uneasy about something, tugging a bit at the picket rope and stomping the ground. The dapple-gray seemed unperturbed. He pulled up the stakes and led the horses back to the campsite, worried that a bear, mountain lion or something worse—Apache—might be in the area.

A soft glow in the sky above the mountain tops hinted that sunrise was approaching, so he went to Bushwa's watch post and, speaking softly, said. "Bushwa, wake up. We'd better get moving." Bushwa did not stir, so Win grabbed a stick and gave him a few sharp pokes in the ribs. His eyes popped open, and he grabbed the Sharps. "What? What?"

"Something is worrying the bay. I brought the horses up. I'm thinking we should saddle up and move on. This place is starting to spook me. It's too quiet here."

"It's night. It's supposed to be quiet."

"Most of the creatures out here are nocturnal. You will hear mountain lions scream at night, hoots of the owls, coyotes howling. There will be animals moving through the brush."

"Nocturnal. Now that's some word. Never heard it. What in blazes are you talking about?"

"Creatures that hunt and feed at night. They thrive in darkness. Most hide out during the day."

"Oh, well, yeah, I guess that's true enough." He clambered to his feet and made his way down the unstable pile of stones that formed a rugged, natural stairway to the outcropping. When he reached solid footing, he stopped and stood quietly for some minutes.

Win could see that Bushwa was taking in the silence, listening for some indication of life beyond their campsite. The blood bay whinnied now and tugged at its lead rope, and the gray started to follow suit.

"I don't like it," Bushwa said. "You're right. Ain't natural out there. We had better saddle up and get the hell out of this place."

"Too late. We have got company." He nodded toward the trail that had led them into the canyon, where three shadowy forms faintly illuminated by the remaining moonlight moved slowly their way. Win could make out rifles carried by two of the men. Then he saw others unmounted, but leading horses, standing in the background. He could not make them out well enough to get a count, but he guessed there would be at least a half dozen. Of course, there could be others farther back or hidden someplace. It appeared they had as much chance of escaping this as they would with hands tied behind their backs facing a firing squad.

"Apaches," Bushwa said. "Ready your rifle."

"There are others. We are taking on ten, maybe more. Let's see if they will talk."

"Do you talk Apache?"

"No, but maybe one of them speaks English."

"I ain't talking to them heathens. You can have a go if you want."

Win figured they had nothing to lose. He laid his rifle down, raised his hand in greeting and walked toward the approaching visitors. The three stopped and one stepped out and continued walking cautiously toward Win. When they were within five paces of each other, Win halted, and the Apache did likewise.

He could make out the Apache's impassive face now, sharp featured with an aquiline nose and eyes that bore into his own. Win did not flinch and met the Indian's stare. He was not an intimidating figure and Win guessed him to be not yet thirty years of age, a half foot shorter than himself but taller than the other two warriors. A wide cloth headband circled his head, and he wore an Army officer's coat that dropped to his hips. Knee-high moccasins covered the legs of loose-fitting cotton britches.

Win said, "My name is Win. Do you speak English?"

"Some. Scout for white eye soldiers from Fort Bliss before they kill my people. I am called Taza."

"Taza, we come in peace and mean no harm. We are going to El Paso. We left the Rio Grande to hunt. We are hungry and have no food. We will return to the river when we find game."

"Not find much here. Soldiers take food while your tribes war. This my hunting party. We find deer and rabbits to take to village. Apache hungry, too. Go south to mountains. We Mescalero. Not war with whites now. Let kill each other, maybe leave our lands."

The man made some sense, Win thought, but eventually there would be survivors to carry on. He was at a loss for words now. This was not a war party, yet they were obviously prepared to fight. What were they here for?

Taza answered his question. "We come for horses. We take horses and go. Not kill if not be fools."

"We may die out here without our horses."

"Maybe. Maybe not. Die if try stop."

An owl hooted from the trees off to one side, and another responded. Taza looked in the direction of the hooting, noticeably unsettled. His companions shared his unease and there was an exchange of intense conversation that Win could not understand.

Suddenly, the strumming of a banjo came from behind him, followed quickly by Bushwa's baritone voice, which was more pleasant in song than in speech. He was singing *Pop Goes the Weasel*. What was the man trying to do?

The owls that had been hooting rose from the trees, flying away, and the warriors watched them and pointed like they had never seen owls before. Win did not know what the Mescalero had against owls, but they appeared not to like the birds.

Taza's eyes fastened on Bushwa now, and Win turned to see his partner sitting on a rotted tree stump, seemingly focused on his music. When he finished that song, he started *Dixie's Land*, the popular tune of the Confederacy.

Taza moved past Win, inching nearer to Bushwa. When he was within less than ten feet from the banjo player, he stopped and stared, apparently mesmerized by the instrument. His two companions soon joined him, and Bushwa moved on to another song. Win had no idea where this was leading, but the Apache visitors had relaxed now and were smiling and nodding their heads in approval.

Minutes later, the remainder of the hunting party drifted into the camp, evidently lured by curiosity. Bushwa performed a twenty-minute concert before he stood and bowed. The Apache just stared at him. Then Taza stepped forward, hand extended, obviously signaling he wanted the banjo.

Bushwa rebelled. "Nope, ain't giving up my banjo to nobody."

"Ban-jo?"

"Yep. This here is called a banjo. You wouldn't know what to do with it. Requires special magic to make its sound."

"Want horses and ban-jo. We go. You no die."

"Ain't giving up my horse neither. I inherited him from Captain McDougal. Decided to call him 'Captain.'"

Taza said. "Take horses and ban-jo."

"Nope. Tell you what. Take me and one horse and the banjo. Leave the red horse for my young friend."

Win protested. "Bushwa. You can't do that. Let them have both horses and the banjo. They can all be replaced."

"I've had this banjo since I learned how to play it. Belonged to my pa. He was pretty much a no-good, but he could pick and strum, I tell you. And I ain't never had a horse like Captain. Ain't letting him out of my sight."

"I just can't do this."

"And what in the hell are you going to do? Do you want to be food for the buzzards and coyotes? I'll make myself valuable to these folks till I think the time is right to move on with Captain and my banjo. Leave word at one of the stables in Las Cruces where I can find you. Just tell them Bushwa will be looking for you. We'll meet up again in less than two months' time. I guarantee it."

He knew that Bushwa could not guarantee anything, but what choice did he have? He was not going to convince the ornery cuss to walk away from his horse and banjo. Of course, a bargain had not been struck yet. His scalp might still be on a warrior's lance before the day was out. He just shrugged.

Taza spoke to Bushwa. "You be Mescalero. Ban-jo bring good spirits. Have Mescalero woman. Friend keep red horse."

"Now, see Win, things are looking better all the time. I get me a woman and be sort of a holy man. I'll be just fine. You help me saddle my horse, and we can talk a spell before I pull out."

He turned back to Taza. "We got a deal if you will throw in a little meat for my friend here."

"Throw in?"

"Leave something for my friend to eat."

Bushwa, the banjo in its leather case and clutched in his hand, walked over to his gelding. "Win, why don't you saddle up for me? I need to go through my saddle bags and get rid of a few things."

The Indians started moving to their own horses. Bushwa continued to talk non-stop while Win saddled the mount. "I kept five eagles just in case they would come in handy someplace. I'm dropping that rawhide pouch with the rest of my gold coins on the ground. Use what you need and hold what's left for me. Just don't put it in no bank. You know how I feel about banks. If we don't join up in a year's time, anything left is yours."

"You said two months."

"That was approximate. If they treat me good, I might take a notion to visit longer."

"I don't like this."

"Don't got to like it. I ain't willing to give up my scalp yet. I been in worse fixes, but I'm inclined to make the best of what's thrown at me, and I might just have a good time." He winked. "Got to be better than walking a thousand miles."

"You've been a good friend to me, Bushwa, like a second pa almost. I'll be worried sick."

"No need to worry. Don't change nothing." He stepped over to Win and extended his hand. They shared a firm grip, and Bushwa said, "And I would have been dang proud to have you for my son."

Win thought he saw the glistening of tears in his partner's eyes, but perhaps they were his own.

Chapter 4

FIVE DAYS LATER, Winston Evans sat astride his blood bay gelding on a hilltop overlooking a vast valley split by the Rio Grande and tugged his hat brim down on his forehead to shield his eyes from the midmorning sun's glare. He could make out what appeared to be two settlements in the distance, a large one on the west side of the river and a smaller cluster of buildings along the east bank and lying a bit south.

His best guess from what Bushwa and other soldiers had told him was that the larger settlement was Mesilla, currently designated as the Capital of the Confederate Territory of Arizona, which included New Mexico Territory. Some of the troops that had joined the Texas volunteers at Valverde had participated in the several battles at the town and nearby Fort Fillmore that concluded with the Confederates overwhelming Union troops and driving them from the area. The Confederate bars and stars now flew over the fort and town.

He would not venture near either Fort Fillmore or Mesilla, but he desperately needed supplies and was starved for something besides an occasional rabbit. He decided to cross the river to Las Cruces, which would take him down from the mountains and through the foothills into the valley, which seemed mostly desert that he had already seen too much of.

The river was shallow now before spring mountain snow thaws from the north brought higher water south, and footing in the riverbed was solid for his mount. When they reached the east bank, he dismounted and pulled on the socks and boots he had removed before the crossing. It was a warm day with winter fading quickly, and he figured the dry heat would soon take care of the britches that were wet to just above the knees.

Now that he had arrived on the fringes of the town, he saw that the inhabitants were spread out over some distance with the small adobe structures at this end separated by enough acreage to support goats, a cow or two, and chickens. He saw patches where gardens had been grown during season, and it appeared that the river bottoms contained some fertile soil before eventually giving way to desert. He saw a wagon road that likely led to commerce and mounted the horse he now called "Buddy" for its tendency to hang close and follow him, more like a dog than horse. Yes, they had bonded these past days.

The dusty, rutted trail led to a string of commercial buildings, almost half of which were saloons or cafes. Most appeared to offer both liquor and food. There were two hotels, but the paintings of half-naked women on signs and walls of the two-story buildings suggested they also doubled as bordellos. The business community seemed spread out as well, with many side streets obviously leading to other establishments.

The town was evidently thriving and seemed unaffected by the war. He noted a large general store on the corner of the next block and counted two barbershops, both advertising baths, both of which he found enticing. He had not shaved since departing the army, and his hair was getting too shaggy for his comfort. He could not recall his last real bath beyond the occasional dunking in river water. Fortunately, he had developed some immunity to his own stench.

He was nearing the end of the commercial buildings along the road when he caught sight of a large livery not more than fifty feet from a two-story frame house, one of the few he had seen that was not adobe. The house was located along the road east of the livery and adjacent to a large expanse of land that merged into the surrounding desert. Fencing suggested they belonged together. As he approached the livery, he read the neatly painted white on red sign above the wide door opening: RUTLEDGE LIVERY & MULES.

Win noticed that another sign was planted in the front yard of the house, and curious, he nudged Buddy ahead. The house was set back some thirty feet from the road and was freshly whitewashed, it appeared. It seemed out of place somehow among the yucca and assorted cactuses that erupted from the sandy, barren earth that surrounded it. A hitching rail along the roadside was vacant, and, if not for a scattering of chickens searching out insects in the yard, the place suggested vacancy. He reined in when he reached the sign that had been erected halfway between the roadside and the house front. It read: RUTLEDGE BED & BOARD.

It would be convenient if his mount could be put up near his lodging in case a speedy exit should be necessary. He also liked the relative isolation of the place from the remainder of the commercial center. He decided to start with the livery and swung his mount back toward the front of that enterprise. He dismounted, hitched Buddy at a rail off to one side, and walked through the opening. At the rear of the long building, he saw someone cleaning stalls, and he strolled down the alleyway between the two rows of stalls.

The stable hand did not seem to be aware of his presence, so as he neared, he called out, "Mister, I'm looking for a place to put up my horse."

The worker looked up, set a pitchfork aside, and walked his way. Win realized instantly that the stable hand was not a "mister," notwithstanding the baggy britches and oversized wool shirt and clodhoppers. The walk and posture did not fit. The woman was taller than the average man and slender as a reed, and as she approached, he saw a very pretty face under the slouch hat.

"Sorry, ma'am. I thought—"

"May I help you?"

"The sign says 'livery,' ma'am. I would like to put up my horse."

"Four bits a day. Includes a few handfuls of grain and full feeding of mixed grass hay. Two and a half dollars will buy a week's stay. We don't take Confederate paper here."

"I can pay in gold coin and would take change in Union coins or dollars. I see there is a boarding house next door with the same name. Is it in business?"

"Yes, of course."

"Do I see the owner at the house?"

"You can see the owner here. One of them. My mother and I own and manage the properties." She stepped forward and extended her hand. "I am Renata Rutledge."

He took her hand, receiving a firmer grip than he anticipated. He hesitated a moment, considering whether he should provide a fictitious name and decided against it. "My name is Winston Evans, but I generally go by Win."

"Well, Mister Evans. Lodging is two dollars a day. That includes a private room with three meals daily. If you don't eat here, there is no credit or refund. We can do a dollar and a half for sleeping only. If you are going to be here anytime at all, the meals are a bargain even if you don't take them all. Baths are available Wednesdays and Saturdays for a dollar each, hot water, soap, and towels furnished. If you are staying long, a weekly bath is requested."

"That sounds more than fair. I am not sure how long I will be here. It might be a few days, or it could be several months."

"Are you looking for work?"

"I am open to the right kind. I am an Iowa farm boy. I don't like being cooped up inside."

"Then you have cleaned stables and handled horses."

"Yes, ma'am, more times than I can count."

"What do you know about mules?"

"I worked for a man that bred and raised the critters. I've done a lot of mule skinning hauling freight in east Texas."

"I thought you were an Iowa boy."

"I left when I was fifteen. That was about five years back after my pa died. My ma was already gone, and my older sister had married and moved to Illinois. I headed south and ended up in Jefferson, Texas. I met Bushwa—my boss—there. He made me kind of a partner in some of his enterprises, and I stayed on."

"But you left?"

"Complicated story, ma'am."

She did not press, and he was grateful for that.

"We can't find help here. All the young men are off to war on one side or the other. I would pay three dollars a day, and you can keep that horse here at no cost. After deduction for room and board, you would clear a dollar a day. That's better than a cowhand or horse wrangler earns in these parts."

"When do I start?"

"After lunch. Find a stall for your critter. I'll show you where we keep the grain and the location of the water pump. You can see the hay stacked out back. I will tell my mother to set another plate for lunch, and we will get a room ready. Get your things together and bring them up to the house. Men sleep upstairs, ladies downstairs—no exceptions without marriage."

She turned and walked briskly out the back door. She had left his head spinning. Things were happening a mite quickly for him to sort out. He had been in town not much more than a half hour and acquired room and board and a new job. He did not know what to think of his employer. She could not be more than a few years older than himself, but she spoke with authority that belied her years.

She seemed a serious sort with coffee-brown eyes that seemed to be constantly searching his own. Her lightly bronzed skin hinted of Spanish or Indian ancestry, but the light, coppery-brown hair tied back in a ponytail suggested Anglo. Bushwa had told him that people out this way were like what Bushwa said cowboys called "son-of-a-bitch stew," a mix of about everything. Some folks cared. Win, whose pedigree was mostly Scotch and English, did not.

Chapter 5

I T HAD BEEN a grueling ride travelling southwest with the Apache hunting party. Obadiah Sparks was surprised at the kind treatment he was receiving from his Indian companions and after a few days no longer feared for his life. Banjo music was required nightly, but he loved an appreciative audience. He did not understand his magic, but the banjo was the dispenser of it.

All the Mescalero now called him "Bush-wa," and he was starting to learn a few Apache words, accepting the fact that his vocabulary would always be severely limited. He would never muster the patience to grasp the cadence and varying grunts and chortles that he gathered meant something. He had joined in the hunts with his Sharps rifle and earned the admiration of the others when he brought down two buffalo cows in a small herd grazing in the foothills of some low mountains.

He had no idea what day of the week it was, but by his count they had been on the trail eight to ten days now taking a zigzag course south. It was midmorning, and they were moving into mountains again now. His best guess was that they had crossed the border into Mexico sometime in the last few days.

Taza reined his mount onto a narrow trail nearly hidden by pine and brush, and Bushwa and Captain fell in behind. The other Apache followed single file with pack animals bearing skin-bound slabs of meat trailing behind. The steep, winding trail, strewn with small stones forced the riders to move at a snail's pace. A mountain stream tumbled over the rocks and down the slope within sight of the party, and they stopped frequently to rest and water the horses, obviously in no rush. Bushwa took it that Taza expected to reach their destination by nightfall.

Midafternoon, the sun's rays broke through the canopy of trees and soon they entered a clearing, and the land began to level until they rode out onto an expanse of tableland already lush with early grasses. He saw plumes of smoke rising in the distance that told him the village was located here. Before the afternoon was out, he expected to know his fate.

As they rode at a walk toward the village, a hodgepodge of dome-shaped wickiups and conical tipis came into sight, he estimated not more than thirty-five scattered about in clusters of three to five. This would not be a huge community, but he knew nothing about the usual size of Apache bands.

Suddenly, women and children were racing across the grassland to greet them, yelling and laughing, obviously happy at the return of the warriors. Taza and his party reined in their horses and waited, most of the warriors dismounting. Soon wives and children were fussing over the married warriors, but Bushwa noticed that there was no kissing or overt displays of affection.

Most of the children broke away quickly, and seven or eight of them started to gather about Bushwa, who remained mounted, watching him with curious wide eyes. He waved, untied the banjo from behind his saddle, and began to sing and strum *The Blue Tail Fly*. His audience, of course, could not understand the words, but they went silent and looked at him with awe and amazement. When he finished, he grinned, revealing the big gap left by his missing front tooth, and the children laughed and raced away.

Taza stepped over to Bushwa. "You follow me. Wives make ready wickiup for you. We eat. Then Coyote Chaser come wickiup, and you talk."

"Who is Coyote Chaser?"

"He tell you."

"He ain't fixing to scalp me or nothing?"

Taza grunted, and Bushwa took that as a laugh. "No scalp. You safe here if no run."

"I ain't going no place." Unless he saw a good opportunity.

The wickiup, was neither the largest nor smallest in the five-lodge cluster, fashioned of poles leaving a ceiling smoke hole and the interior thatched with yucca leaves, reeds and grasses woven between the poles to ward off wind and rain. There were several blankets and a buffalo robe stretched out on a skin-covered floor. Added to his own bedroll, he figured these were the best sleeping accommodations he had been offered since departing Jefferson months ago. It occurred to him that his chances of getting killed were no greater, and possibly much less, than where he had been headed with the volunteers. He hoped young Win Evans was doing half as well.

He did not like turning Captain out with the horses in the Apache remuda, but Taza had assured him that the horse was his and not subject to any warrior's claim. Taza told him that the herdsmen took the critters to the best grasses and that the horses would be protected. Bushwa knew that horses were the measure of wealth for most Indians he had ever encountered, and he convinced himself that his dapple-gray gelding was being well cared for, and, besides, what choice did he have?

Taza had showed him the male wasting grounds beyond the village where he could empty bowels and bladder. Bushwa had a strong stomach, but the stench almost gagged him. He would have much preferred a private privy near his wickiup but supposed that would be asking for a bit too much. He would avoid the place as much as possible and find trees to water in the timber when he could. At least he would not be sharing with the women, but from the odor drifting in from the north he guessed their grounds were not too far distant.

He ate with Taza's family, which included two quite attractive young wives and three children, two boys and a girl less than five years old, all of whom shared the largest structure in the cluster. Taza's lodge was a tipi more like those Bushwa had seen in the occasional Comanche village he had visited during the army's journey across Texas. He learned that the wives were sisters, which evidently was not uncommon. An older man and woman were included in the group, and he finally concluded they were the wives' parents.

He was uncertain of the kinship of the other younger woman present, but he found her pretty enough, stouter, and bustier than the other two, and he liked her laughing eyes that seemed to look back at him with some interest. It seemed like years since he had bedded a woman, and he supposed that she looked all the better for it.

He could not complain about the food served by the women, who did not eat until after the men had finished. Roasted venison and something akin to cornbread. He could have handled some dessert, but maybe Apaches were not familiar with that necessity. It might be a spell before he ate cobbler or pie again. He noted that the un-attached woman served his food, and she had offered a big smile when he nodded his thanks.

Later, Bushwa, tired from his journey and with a full belly from his meal, napped in his wickiup. It was not sundown yet when he was awakened by Taza's voice from outside. "Bush-wa."

He rolled off his blankets and scrambled to his knees. "Yeah, what is it?"

"Bring Coyote Chaser."

What in blazes was he talking about? "I ain't got no coyotes in here. But come on in."

The deerskin flap that covered the door opening was pulled aside, and a short, wiry man ducked his head and stepped into the wickiup followed by Taza. The visitor had silvery hair controlled by a cloth band, but Bushwa would not place him at more than fifty years old.

Taza said, "This Coyote Chaser. Him talk white tongue good."

Bushwa got to his feet. "Howdy, Coyote Chaser. Pleased to make your acquaintance." He extended his hand, and the visitor responded with a quick grasp.

"Hello, Mister Bushwa. My pleasure."

Taza said, "Coyote Chaser di-yin. Tell you much. I go." The chief turned and disappeared through the entryway.

Bushwa was uncertain what he was to say to the man he towered over in front of him. The Indian was sure wickiup size, he thought. His own head brushed the ceiling at its peak. This fella had plenty of clearance. "Afraid I can't offer you a drink, but I suppose we could sit down if you want to palaver a spell."

"That would be good. I have much to say."

The men both sat down cross-legged on blankets facing each other.

Coyote Chaser said, "During the months ahead, I am to teach you the ways of our Mescalero people and about your responsibilities here."

Months? Responsibilities? Bushwa did not like the sound of either word. "You don't talk like no Apache, but I am listening."

"I am what you would probably call a half-breed. My father was a trader and my mother Mescalero. I lived among the whites until I was thirteen years old. I attended a mission school in Albuquerque. I learned to read and still acquire books when I can."

"Never read a book. Can make out a few words and sign my name."

"Anyway, when my father died, my mother found her way back to her people. Her family was in the Fox subband, and Taza is one of four chiefs of this band. Most Apache bands are made up of relatives, and the Mescalero consist of many bands."

"Makes sense, I guess. So the folks here are mostly cousins and such?"

"You could say that, but it gets complicated, because many of the men formerly belonged to other bands. When a man first marries, he goes to live with the band of the wife's parents."

"Okay, but I ain't married. What the devil am I doing here?"

"You will be married soon, and I am to train you to be a di-yin."

"Taza called you that. And I ain't sure about this marrying stuff. I done that twice already and don't know if either of the witches divorced me. They run off someplace."

"Yes, I am the coyote di-yin for this rancheria."

"I don't know what the hell that means. Is it like a medicine man or such?"

"That would be near enough. But the main duty of the di-yin is to ward off bad spirits. The coyote can be such a spirit if molested or disturbed and we do not wish them near the rancheria. They can bring an accident or even the coyote sickness, which can cause blindness, disfigurement, crossed eyes or disabling cramps to hands and legs. When those come, I know coyote ceremonies that I use to help. Care must be taken with all the dog family, but the fox is least harmful and can even be a friend."

"And if I am a di-yin, what do I do?"

"The most feared of all the creatures that possess powers is the owl, one reason that most Apache fear the night and generally will avoid venturing into the darkness if possible. Certainly, it is not the time to engage in battle. Owls signal the presence of ghosts. They can be a sign that the hearer or one of his family is going to die or get owl sickness where they cannot move or faint or become disoriented. It is the ghost who controls the owl that does this."

"Always sort of liked owls myself. Never got no sickness."

"You, as a di-yin would try to keep the owl ghosts away and create ceremonies that cure the sickness or ward off the danger of death. Some of this will take time and my guidance. If you meet the challenge, you will be the most powerful di-yin of all, and you and your family will never do without."

"You make me sound like some dang preacher or something."

"A good analogy."

"Don't know what analogy is, but it sounds like this is a racket I could take to."

"I would prefer you not think of it that way."

"Do you believe all this stuff about ghosts and spirits and the like>"

"It doesn't matter what I believe. Who knows anything for certain? I just want to help my people. I have made my place here among my mother's family, and I am useful in the rancheria as both di-yin and interpreter."

Slick. This feller is slick, Bushwa thought. Well, he would play the game if it would save his scalp. It sounded like fun. "You mentioned a wife."

Chapter 6

COYOTE CHASER'S EYES would be considered brown in the daylight, but as the wickiup darkened from the beginning of a setting sun, Bushwa thought he saw them taking on a fiery white glow—like the coyote's night eyes. He shivered and turned serious. Maybe those damned ghosts did hang around Apache country.

"Yes, the wife. You have met her. She is Taza's sister. Her name is Nascha. It means "Owl" in our language."

"Owl? But Apaches is afraid of owls. And you are thinking I'm going to be scaring off the creatures. I gather she was the one fixing the grub along with Taza's wives."

"Yes, she is believed to have owl powers, also, but a woman's powers are not accepted by many. That is why Taza brought you here. When you strummed your banjo and played, two hooting owls flew away. Taza took that as a sign that you had powers. He decided you were the perfect mate for Nascha. Your powers joined will give our rancheria nearly insurmountable protection against owl ghosts, he believes. You will be known as Owl Man among the People."

"Why do they think this Nascha has owl powers?"

Coyote Chaser said. "In her twelfth summer, she found an owl with an injured wing in the forest. She carried it back to the rancheria. The bird did not protest in her arms, but when she arrived at the lodges, the people were terrified and did not know what to do. They did not want the owl in their midst, and they dared not kill it or abandon it now. The consequences could destroy them."

"Yeah, I can see they might think that. Either one could make the dang ghosts mad."

"Her father and mother—we do not speak the names of the dead—constructed a wickiup out of sight of the rancheria, and Nascha lived there with the owl for over two months. The parents brought food to her and left it not far from the wickiup. The girl did not once cry or complain. She shared her food with the owl while the creature healed. One day, it flew away, and only then did Nascha cry. She is a kind and gentle soul. She laughs much. She will be a good wife."

"You sound like this is a done deal."

Bushwa

"I highly recommend you consider it such."

The tone of Coyote Chaser's voice made Bushwa's decision for him. "Okay. When does this happen?"

"Tomorrow night. It is usually expected that the new husband pay a price for his new wife to her family, horses, or something of value. Her parents have journeyed to the other world, so that is less important now."

"Got one horse. Ain't giving him up."

"I will speak with Taza on your behalf. He is fascinated with your banjo music. Perhaps, you would play and sing some music before you take your new bride to the wickiup."

"I would be glad to do that. Is there a ceremony or anything that declares us husband and wife?"

"No, it is not like a white man's wedding. After your music, she will come to you and follow you to your wickiup."

This did not sound so bad. "And after that I get all the privileges of a husband, if you know what I mean?"

Coyote Chaser's solemn face finally cracked a closed-mouth smile. "I know what you mean, and the answer is 'yes,' but Coyote demands that you treat her kindly and gently."

"I wouldn't hurt a woman, but I don't understand."

"I will teach you the significance of Coyote to the People in the days ahead. He is difficult to grasp because he is tricky and can be both good and evil. It is taken as a truth among the Apache that many years ago, Coyote found a beautiful woman and wanted to use her woman cave. He could be a scoundrel and lusted for many women. He led her into the woods and just when he was ready to mount her, he saw that the woman cave was full of teeth and was frightened. Instead of entering her he put in a stick, but she chewed it all up."

Bushwa said, "Now you ain't exactly heating up my blood with this tale."

"But allow me to finish. After the stick disappeared, Coyote put a stone in the woman cave, and it broke all the teeth, making it smooth like the women we have come to know. And the woman said to Coyote, 'Now, you have made me valuable. Men will pay horses for me, and they will do many things for permission to enter my woman cave.' Coyote was a rascal and did many bad things at the beginning, but sometimes he tried to help, and because of him we have many things we could not do without."

Bushwa said, "Well, I sure enough thank him for that."

The next evening, shortly after sundown the Apache from all the lodges began to gather at a fire encircled by large stones just outside the rancheria clusters. Bushwa noticed that all the men gathered at one side with the woman congregating on the opposite. The sexes seemed to keep a healthy distance from each other out in public, and he could not recall seeing any hugs or handholding between couples since his arrival. He guessed he had better keep an eye out for such things if he did not want to cause a fuss.

He stood not far from the fire with his banjo's neck clutched in one hand and the rim of the head resting in the crook of his other elbow, waiting for the audience members to claim places. He saw his bride-to-be arrive and join the women. She cast him a quick look before she turned her head away. Tonight, she was attired in buckskins that clung to her a bit and showed she had a female body that was rounded where it should be. She was far from a skinny little thing, but he had always preferred women with a little meat on their bones. Darned if he was not getting horny as a billy goat just thinking about her.

The gathering suddenly went silent at the hooting of several owls in a cluster of cedars to the south. He could hear the mumbling and whispering sweeping through the crowd and sensed their fear, taking that as his cue to start. He began strumming and strolling around the circle singing, "Queen Victoria's very sick . . . Prince Albert's got the measles . . . the children have the whooping cough . . . and pop goes the weasel."

He knew thirty or forty verses from different versions of the tune, all ending, of course, with "pop goes the weasel." When he reached the children sitting together at the far end of the fire circle, he danced a little jig as he sang one of the verses, and when he said "pop goes the weasel," he tossed his banjo in the air, catching it easily, having performed the stunt many times. The children loved it and laughed. They weren't worried about the owls.

Bushwa, knowing that no one other than Coyote Chaser would understand the words, performed a dozen different verses before he was finished, and by the end, the children and a few of the mothers were yelling "pop" when he reached that point in the song. Then there was silence. He waited for the hooting of the owls to come from the darkness, but thankfully they had either gone quiet or flown away because of the noise. He could see that the Mescalero had calmed now and some of the men had chosen to settle on the ground. Maybe he had earned a feather or something.

He continued playing and singing for another half hour, sticking with the lively songs. There was no applause, but his audience was mesmerized. When he finished his last tune, he bowed and waved before he started to walk away. He stopped when the audience began to chant, "Pop, pop." He swung around and performed an encore with another dozen verses, and now most of the adults were joining in with the "pops."

When he stepped away from the fire circle, Bushwa was met by Taza. Nascha stood a few paces behind him. Taza said, "Owl Man go to wickiup. Nascha follow. She be what white man call wife, and you husband." Taza continued to the fire circle, and Bushwa started walking toward his wickiup at the far end of the rancheria. He could hear Taza's voice speaking to the assembled tribespeople but had no notion what he was saying and did not care. The woman trailing behind him was all he could think about. He entered the wickiup first, figuring that was likely the proper thing in this place. It was dark inside except for a stream of moonlight finding its way through the airhole at the peak.

He saw her shadowy form and realized she was letting herself down upon his bed of blankets. She was silently slipping out of her garments. As his eyes got accustomed to the darkness, he realized she was naked and waiting for him. He decided preliminaries must not be necessary and quickly abandoned his moccasins, britches, and shirt and lay down beside her. She did not move, apparently waiting. He was more than ready, and since he had no idea of what was expected of an Apache warrior, he did not waste more time.

Then he encountered an obstacle. He had never had a virgin before, and he thought of the woman's cave with teeth, but she helped and then it was good. Later, they coupled again, and she seemed more interested, and just before sunrise she became almost demanding. He was totally confused about this woman and his future with the Apache, but life among the People so far had not been all that bad—tonight had been dang good. He would make the best of it for now.

Chapter 7

April 1862

AFTER OVER SIX weeks working at the livery, Win Evans was still an enigma to Renata Rutledge. He had been a godsend to the sundry Rutledge enterprises, working willingly from dawn to dusk and beyond if necessary. She had yet to find a chore he could not handle competently. Not only was he at ease working with the horses and mules, but he had also mastered the rare art of enticing a mare in the breeding chute to allow the donkey jack to mount her and plant his seed for the future mule offspring.

Win was a skilled carpenter as well and had embarked on repairs of whatever needed fixing at both house and stable. Moreover, her mother, Martina, adored the young man, doting on him like a child. Sometimes to her daughter's annoyance. She supposed her mother had never experienced a man helping her clear the table and washing dishes before. He could even help with the cooking.

But he never talked about much besides the weather, never offered a hint about his background beyond an occasional remembrance of his Iowa farm days or a work experience in Jefferson. She had not a clue about how he came to be in Las Cruces or his feelings about the war. He was hiding something. But what?

She could not deny that he was a handsome devil, quite pleasant to a woman's eye, but she was older, having recently turned twenty-three. She supposed she was not that much older, but she felt it. She had been a widow for nearly two years now after losing her soldier husband to an Apache arrow in a skirmish near the Mexican border. She supposed a respectable woman would identify herself as "Missus Wieland" now, but she was not one to seek respectability and had reclaimed her maiden name quickly.

She had married the dashing Captain Joshua Wieland when she was seventeen, captured by his charm and confident manner, only to learn that in private he was insecure, cruel and physically abusive, the latter subdued when she threatened to slice his throat with a butcher knife while he slept if he ever struck her again. She decided he had married her as an exhibit for promotion.

Men his age should be married, should they not? She was no longer a virgin but just barely past that milestone. They had been intimate no more than a dozen times during a nearly three-year marriage, and those moments had been clumsy and unsatisfying. His prolonged absences in the field had not helped, but she came to realize that his preferences were for the male sex, which would not do for an ambitious soldier.

She did come to pity the man, but not so much that she would remain with him. She returned home to work in her parents' businesses a year before he was killed in action. She attended his funeral at Fort Bliss but did not apply for a widow's pension, preferring to erase that chapter of her life, and it did not seem right somehow to profit from a man she had intended to eventually divorce. Oh, how foolish we could be in our youth. She hoped better judgment was coming with age.

And now she was a spy for the Union Army, taking the risk of dying at the end of a rope. Her dilemma was that she was having difficulty with surveillance at locations where a woman's presence would draw too much attention. Also, her contact had been concerned at his last visit that he was being followed. He feared that further calls would place them both at risk. She must find another way to get messages to him.

She required assistance. Could Win Evans be the answer? The Union generals hoped to recapture Fort Fillmore and Mesilla by summer, Fort Bliss to the south as well. She was the information link, chosen because a woman seemed an unlikely accomplice in an intelligence scheme, even though her father was a Union colonel fighting along the east coast at last report. Few locals were aware of this, however.

She decided that she would talk with Win after lunch. They would saddle horses, and she would show him more of the Rutledge property. He likely had no idea of the potential of the family enterprises and extent of their holdings.

Chapter 8

RENATA'S MOTHER, MARTINA, was an attractive woman, a half foot shorter than her daughter and petite. Win thought her to be in her early forties and had become fond of her during his stay at the boarding house. Unlike her rather solemn daughter, she was a cheery person with a seemingly perpetual smile on her face and spoke near perfect English with a thick Spanish accent.

This morning Martina emerged from the kitchen with a tray bearing a cup of steaming coffee, a plate filled with a stack of hotcakes, and another with slices of bacon and fried eggs. She set the coffee and dishes in front of Win who was the only guest seated at the dining table.

Martina said, "You eat alone today, Win. Renata took her coffee and said she had bookkeeping in the livery office to tend to. Miss May does not teach school today and said she would be eating later. And I do not think Mister Donalds feels well this morning."

That meant Frank Donalds had gone on a drunken binge the night before, but he was generally not at the first breakfast at six o'clock anyway. Win had only seen the occupant of the room adjacent to his on one occasion, a skinny, sallow-faced man with glassy eyes who did not acknowledge his greeting. Ruth May, a fortyish woman who generally joined him at the early breakfast, on the other hand, was a friendly and outgoing sort who carried the conversation most mornings. Win liked her and thought the buxom, auburn-haired woman was rather attractive.

He and the other two were the only long-term guests. There were two more rooms on each floor, and the other men's rooms occasionally had an occupant for a night or two, but he had yet to see another paying guest on the main floor, where Renata and Martina both maintained rooms.

Martina sat down across the table while Win poured hot maple syrup over the hotcakes. "Do you mind my company while you eat?" she asked.

"Of course not. I always enjoy talking with you."

"I know Renata seems to be a bit—I don't know how to say this—cold with you."

Win hesitated as he ate a forkful of the hotcakes. "She is just businesslike. She is my boss. I understand that. She tells me what she expects. I do it. She has not been unkind. I like working for her."

"I am so glad to hear you say that. She needs you here. I do, also. I hope you will not be leaving soon."

"I have no plans to move on right now, but I do have responsibilities I will need to deal with sometime in the future. I will try not to surprise you, though, and give plenty of notice."

Martina said, "You have not hinted how you feel about the war. My husband is a colonel in the Union cavalry. He resigned his commission some years back but rejoined when the war broke out. He is somewhere in the east, but I have not heard from him for months. I pray that he still lives. Our business has been harmed because of our known Union sympathies. We are despised by some, and our friends, even those who share our views, shy away from being seen with us. Renata believes most folks in Las Cruces support the Union, but many are intimidated by the Confederate takeover of Mesilla and Fort Fillmore."

She was obviously fishing for his view of the conflict that had engulfed the nation. This was tricky ground. He was not ready to disclose that he was a deserter from the

Rebel army. He still suffered some guilt about that even though he did not support the cause.

Win said, "I will tell you this much. I want to see the Union preserved. I oppose slavery. I come from Iowa, and if I had lived there when the war broke out, I would be wearing Union blue. That does not mean I worship the North. During the years I lived in Jefferson, Texas I got downright embarrassed about the arrogance and snobbery of a lot of Northerners and the way they looked down on people from the South. I could see why men were willing to support the rebellion. It is a complicated thing that would take somebody smarter than me to understand."

"Would you help the Union if given the opportunity?"

Gunshots from the direction of the livery kept him from answering a question he would have had to ponder. He pushed back his chair and leaped to his feet. "My rifle is upstairs."

"I have a loaded Henry my husband gave to us before he left for the war. He didn't take it because it was one of the first made, he said." She raced into the kitchen where she had secreted the gun and returned and handed it to Win. He grabbed the rifle, raced out the door and headed for the stable, where the gunfire continued but was intermittent now. He saw two horses hitched on the railing in front of the livery, so he went to the side entryway which was directly across from Renata's office.

He pulled the door ajar just enough to peer inside. The office door was wide open, but the tiny room had apparently been vacated. It was deathly still now, and then he heard a male voice with a Southern accent coming from the alleyway to his right at the rear of the livery. He levered a cartridge into the rifle's chamber and stepped into the building, his view obstructed by the plank walls covering the stalls on each side that rose above his head a good foot and furnished tunnel-like access.

As he crept toward the alleyway, he could make out the speaker's voice clearly. "Ya'll kilt Hank, Yankee bitch. Now it's your turn to die."

Renata said, "You are a fool. You and your friend started the shooting. I was just defending myself."

"You are in Confederate territory, woman, and that makes spying for the Yankees treason against your country. We was under orders to put a stop to your treachery."

"The Confederacy is not my country and never will be."

"If that's all you got to say, I ain't got more time to waste and best be on my way. Time for you to say your prayers."

Win hollered, "Hold it mister." He stepped into the alleyway, his Henry held waist- high and uncertain where his target might be. He caught a glimpse of Renata on the floor, raised up on one elbow when a heavy man dressed in a Confederate jacket and cap and faded denims turned toward him with pistol raised to fire. Win squeezed the Henry's trigger, praying lead would strike its target from its awkward position. The man grunted and stumbled but then straightened, readying to fire his weapon with a shaky hand. By this time Win had levered another cartridge and fired again. The would-be killer got off a wild shot before the gun dropped from his hand. He stared at Win with disbelieving eyes before he collapsed on the dirt floor.

"My God," Renata said. "I didn't know you were there. You saved my life. In another minute, I would have been dead."

"Your mother and I heard the gunfire from the house."

"There were just the two. They came in hollering my name, and at this time of the morning, I figured that likely meant trouble. I keep my rifle near the desk, so I grabbed it and took a step out into the alleyway. When I saw the men in gray, I ducked back in the office. The man you shot said I was under arrest and that I should come out with my hands raised. I went back out, told them they were trespassers and to get off our property. His companion, a smaller, younger man, fired at me with his pistol, and I took him down with my Volcanic. But then it jammed—they are prone to do that, you know?"

He did not and shrugged and she continued. "Anyhow, I made a run for the rear and dodged the big man's bullets, and then I tripped over a water bucket and fell like a clumsy clown. That's when he ran me down. I don't know how much you heard, but he told me I could still come peaceably, and he would take me to Confederate headquarters in Mesilla. I told him to go to hell."

Win said, "I missed that part, but it doesn't matter right now. We've got two dead bodies we need to do something with. I am going to close and bar the stable doors till we get this figured out. Why don't you head over to the house and let your mother know you are alright? She has got to be crazed with worry. I'll drag the corpses into an empty stall for now and then I will be over to finish breakfast."

She stared at him in disbelief. "Breakfast?"

"Yes, ma'am, you interrupted my breakfast."

"I'm sorry," she said sarcastically.

"Yeah, now I will have to eat my hotcakes cold." He headed toward the front of the stable and the lifeless form crumpled in front of the open door. He looked back after he reached the big double doors and saw that Renata had disappeared. After peering outside, he exited and retrieved the two horses hitched at the rail. He led the horses inside and pulled the door shut.

Renata's absence gave him a chance to catch his breath. He needed some time to think this out. He had just killed a man who appeared to be a Confederate soldier and aligned himself with a woman accused of being a Union spy. If he were identified and captured, he was virtually guaranteed a firing squad or a noose about his neck.

Chapter 9

I T TOOK RENATA a spell to calm her mother who had been convinced that her only child had been killed, but she seemed to have collected herself now. Martina Rutledge was a strong woman, ordinarily tough as nails, but tended to unravel when her daughter faced a crisis.

They waited at the dining table for Win to return. "You told me he wanted to finish breakfast," Martina said.

"It was a strange thing to say, but yes. He complained that his hotcakes would be cold of all things. And he got bossy with me like he had forgotten that I am his employer. He was telling me what to do."

Martina laughed. "It is good for you not to have a man back down from you sometimes."

"I am grateful he was here, and I can't forget he saved my life. I guess I was just taken aback by his sudden change. I had always thought of him as a boy."

"To me, he is a boy, but a strong and handsome one. If I did not have a husband, I just might be stalking that boy."

"Madre, you can be disgusting sometimes. You are old enough to be his mother."

"Well, my daughter is only a few years older than Win and seems to be blind to his attributes."

"I am not blind, and I like him well enough. But the last thing I am looking for is a man. What are we going to tell him? He has been pulled into this mess now. I don't even know where he stands on the war."

"He as much as told me that he is with the Union, but he appears torn about some things. He must be told the truth now, and we can hope that he will share more of himself. There are decisions to be made, and I am guessing we have no more than today to make them."

"Yes, there has been a leak somewhere, and the Confederates have learned that I am a spy. When those men do not deliver me to their superior, others will come. We must leave, but the animals—"

"You must go. I will stay. I have not been directly involved and can claim ignorance. Your aunt Camila will send her boys to help with chores for now, but I cannot ask them to tend to breeding of the jacks and mares. You may not raise many mules this year, but we can hold the herd together unless the Confederates confiscate it. When the Union retakes New Mexico and Southwest Texas, you will be able to return."

"But that could be months or years."

"I will be here. If I am asked, I know nothing of the soldiers who came here. I just know that you disappeared."

They both started when the back door opened, and Win walked in carrying four rifles and several belts of ammunition. He laid his collection on the floor along one wall. "I stashed their pistols under the haystack at the rear of the stable. We will need to do something with all the weapons. After I finish my breakfast, I will bury the two men in the stall where I dragged them. We don't dare toss them outside. I will spread some straw and move a horse or mule in there with food and water. Whoever takes over livery chores should care for the critter in the stall and not turn it out for a few days. They should not clean the stall. It's not likely the bodies will be found there."

Martina got up and said, "Fresh hotcakes, bacon, and eggs will be ready soon. I will warm your coffee, too."

"I would appreciate that, ma'am."

"I can help with burying the men and finding an animal for the stall," Renata said.

"I brought their mounts into the stable. We can't leave the horses here. They have CSA brands on their hips. We will leave right after sunset and take the horses with us, turn them loose somewhere not far from town. They'll find their way to somebody who will claim them. I'll bet they won't be turned back to the army, brands or not."

"You said we are leaving after sundown. Both of us? Together?"

"Well, I am not sticking around for my hanging. I don't know about you but consider yourself invited."

"Where will we go? I have reasons that I can't go far from here."

"Well, once we are clear of town, you can go wherever you want. I won't have a rope tied to you. On the other hand, if we do a little truth telling, I might hang close, too, for a spell."

There was a long silence during which Martina served Win a fresh breakfast. Renata watched while he ate, amazed at how calm he appeared to be after all that had happened this morning. In a few hours' time, Win Evans had been transformed from boy to man in her eyes. He stopped before forking another portion of syrup-drenched hotcakes into his mouth and looked at her.

His cobalt-blue eyes fastened on hers as if searching for something. Obviously, he was aware that she had been staring at him. She refused to flinch but was relieved when he returned his focus to breakfast.

When Win finished eating, he sipped his coffee a moment before tossing a look over his shoulder and calling to her mother in the kitchen. "Martina, could you join us at the table. Storytime."

Martina came in and took a chair beside him, giving his shoulder a gentle squeeze as she sat down. Both now faced Renata on the opposite side of the table. Renata found herself annoyed by her mother's familiar behavior with Win. Martina was a toucher by nature, but she had adored Win since his arrival and made too much of a fuss over him as far as Renata was concerned. Madre was married after all and a generation older than Win, although she and her mother were occasionally mistaken for sisters by strangers.

Win's voice yanked her back to the dilemma they faced. "Time to lay the cards on the table," Win said, "even if it takes some time. I'll go first. I am a deserter from the Confederate Army." He quickly gave a summary of his friendship with Bushwa Sparks, their desertion of the Rebel encampment and the altercation with the Apache. "I came here to wait for Bushwa to show up. I am holding some money for him if he does. I think he would eventually find his way to your livery if he is still alive, but I have serious doubts about that."

Martina said, "I am not leaving. It is my renegade daughter they will be seeking. I told Renata that I will know nothing, only that she has disappeared. I will be here if your friend shows up. We can hide the money, bury it perhaps, if you trust me to take custody of it."

He turned to Martina and took her hand. "Of course, I trust you, and I would be grateful if you would do this. I have funds of my own that I will take with us."

Renata thought she might vomit at the sight of these two fawning over each other. And her poor father was at war, likely under fire in some godforsaken place, if he still lived. Her mother should be ashamed.

Renata wanted some questions answered and diverted their attention from each other. "Very well, Win. Your story explains things, and I have no way to verify its truth."

"Renata," Martina said, "that is rude and uncalled for to suggest otherwise."

"That's alright, Martina," Win said, "I can hardly believe it myself." He switched his attention to Renata. "Now, I think it is only fair for you to show your cards.

Those men were not making a social call, and I heard some talk of spying."

"I am a spy for the Union Army. I was contacted because my father is a Union officer, and it was thought that because I am a woman, I would not be suspected. I have since learned that there are many women performing this work in the war, a large number being employed by the Pinkerton Detective Agency. Unfortunately, I am not being paid."

"But what can you learn from here?"

"There is a network of people involved. We are to track movement of the Confederate troops, try to get troop count estimates, that sort of thing. The objective is to assist the Union with the timing for the Army to retake Fort Fillmore and Mesilla, as well as Fort Bliss to the south, which would effectively reestablish control of El Paso. The livery makes it convenient for my contacts to reach me on the pretext of doing business. This is especially helpful to couriers from Fort Bliss. It is my job to send summaries of my information west to Tucson. Union troops will come from California when the retaking happens. They are already congregating there."

"It sounds complicated."

Martina said, "You get word to your people that I will continue to take messages here."

"Madre, it would be too dangerous. I do not think so. But I will get word back to you as to how I may be contacted. You must focus on keeping our land and businesses in operation. My cousins will help, but I can only expect them to work a short time without pay."

Win said, "You are short of funds?"

Renata said, "It is a problem. You have seen that we have work for three or four men here, but we have barely taken in enough since the war to pay your wages and buy food for ourselves and the animals. There are shortages of everything, especially since the Confederates took control. And we are what some would call land poor."

"Thanks to my living arrangements here, I haven't spent more than a dollar of my wages, and I have other money saved up. I can loan you three hundred dollars, all in gold coins, and still have money left to carry me for some months. I'll bet there aren't many businesses in town anxious to take Confederate graybacks. And then there is Bushwa's gold if you become desperate. He would understand if he ever turns up, and if he does not, it is mine. Regardless, I would be responsible for reimbursing him, and he gave me permission to use the money if I needed it."

Renata said, "No, I do not know when we can pay you back. And I do not want to be obligated."

Martina placed a hand on Win's shoulder. "Pay no attention to her. I will accept your loan. We can survive many months with that and whatever income we can bring in. We will prosper again when Andrew comes home. The land that surrounds us here includes ten thousand acres. It is part of a Spanish land grant that came from my family. My sister Camila owns an adjacent ten thousand acres. My father said that Las Cruces has no place to grow but on our land. We must hold it. The portion that is not needed for our purposes will have a market someday. This will be an investment for you."

Martina gently placed her fingers on the back of his neck and pulled his head toward her pressing her lips to his cheek before releasing her grasp. "Thank you, my son. Thank you more than I can say."

Renata sighed. When had she ever won an argument with her mother? She hated the sense of obligation that came with the loan. Still, they would have been fools to turn it down. Better that her mother accepted the funds than she. "Win, I guess we are going to leave together tonight, but I am still confused about your intentions."

"Well, I don't want to get too far away from my money, and my heart and head tell me I am blue, not gray. I thought I would stick around and see if a certain Union spy could use an assistant."

"You would help me?"

"Yes, ma'am, if you will let me."

Renata thought a moment. Folks in the area knew her and would recognize her if she went to many places. It was unlikely anyone could identify Win. "Yes," she said. "I would be grateful for your help."

"I knew it," Martina said, a big smile spreading on her face. "I can sleep more easily now."

Win said, "I had better find me a shovel and get to work."

Chapter 10

WIN AND RENATA, mounted on his gelding, Buddy, and Spirit, her black-baldface mare, crossed the Rio Grande in the shallows that Win had discovered when he first approached Las Cruces. A rare cloud cover hovered above offering them a shield of blackness. Before crossing, they had released the saddled Confederate horses into a goat pen behind a small adobe house.

"The goats are already making a fuss," Renata had said. "Santiago will be out soon to check on them. We must ride."

Now that they had reached the west bank, the two riders were slipping back into boots and britches. Win had worried about the logistics of crossing since he did not want to start the journey soaked. Fortunately, when he told her that the water would probably reach thigh-high if they remained mounted, Renata had suggested they remove the affected garments. She had added, "Since it's dark anyhow."

"I did not explain," she said, "when I suggested we leave the horses in the goat pen. My friends, Santiago and Emilia, live in that little adobe house with their six children. They are very poor, especially since the Confederate takeover. He will find a place to market the saddles, and I am guessing he will know where to sell the horses. We made him a wealthy man this night. Santiago is a hard worker and a good man. He deserves a windfall."

"I figured you had a reason for choosing the place."

"I am almost lost on this side of the river until I find the Butterfield Trail. I hope you have a notion of where we are headed. Perhaps we could get a bit of sleep before we talk about our plans. We are near the Organ Mountains which bound Las Cruces from several directions."

Win said, "I did not know what they were called but I passed by or through these west of the river on my journey to your town. I saw a place in the foothills about an hour's ride from here at a night pace that should suit us for now if I can find it in the dark."

"You lead the way."

They headed west moving quickly into the foothills, following a narrow trail that snaked between rugged hillocks and through dry arroyos covered with sand and small stones. Craggy walls and spires of shadowy stone were visible even in the darkness now. Win reined Buddy in and dismounted.

"I am looking for a deer path that forks off the trail toward the slopes. It isn't far from here. I remember that big boulder that looks almost like a giant bell." He pointed to a rock formation not more than fifteen feet off the trail. "I rode up the path, looking for water, figuring there was a chance since animals traveled it. I was lucky. I struck water."

Several minutes later, he picked up the path, mounted, and reined his gelding up the narrow trail that gradually sloped higher toward the mountain's face. Soon they reached a granite escarpment protruding from the base of the mountains that towered above them.

"Watch your step here. It's wet and slippery from a stream that comes out through a passageway and feathers out over the rocks."

"A passageway to where?" Renata said.

"A little box canyon not more than a hundred feet deep. A freshwater spring seeps from a place in the wall and forms a nice pool before it overflows and heads toward the opening and on down the slope. That little pond we just passed is where most of the wild creatures drink.

You will want to dismount now and lead your mare along the edge of the stream. I will make a sharp turn shortly and will disappear for a moment but there is plenty of room once you make the turn."

He led Buddy through the entrance, which he and the horse had passed through nearly two months earlier. The passageway was a good ten feet wide and not quite half occupied by shallow, flowing water, and the crevice extended only a dozen feet before breaking into the blind canyon. He led the gelding out onto the grass made possible by the moisture dripping at multiple locations off the rock walls.

When Renata joined him, she said, "I can't see much, but it seems like a perfect hiding place. It should be invisible from below."

"It is. I am thinking we should headquarter here. I doubt if many white men know of the place. Our biggest risk would be Apache."

"With all the military action near Mesilla and Las Cruces, they seem to be steering clear of the area lately. I guess they used to attack the towns regularly before Fort Fillmore was constructed by the Army a dozen years ago. We did not move to Las Cruces until the Army had a post here."

"Let's find a place to set up camp. We can stake the horses out near the stream and lay out our bedrolls and grab some shuteye. In the morning, if we decide that we will be here a spell, we can make a better shelter with the canvas tarp you brought and find a suitable place for a fire. We've got a coffee pot and a Dutch oven at least, and your mother sent us enough food to last a few days."

"She sent enough biscuits to feed us for more than a few."

"I love her biscuits, but they won't be the same without her cherry jam."

"She wanted to send it along with a wagonload of supplies, but we couldn't carry any more without a pack-horse. Besides, we can get more supplies at one of our first stops, Butterfield's Rough and Ready Station."

"Never heard of it."

"Not a day's ride on the Butterfield Trail, probably less from here. I need to get word to somebody there."

He was curious but decided not to press for too much information yet. He could let her operate under a cloak of secrecy, if she wished, for as long as he was unaffected by it.

"His name is Bodaway," she said. "It means 'fire maker,' I am told. He is Mescalero and a critical courier in our chain. And I trust him. He is not the faulty link."

"Mescalero. They are the ones who captured Bushwa."

"Not Bodaway. He has worked for the Army for a dozen years. He scouted for my father just before Papa retired from the cavalry the first time."

"Would he be able to tell me anything about a band that includes a leader named Taza?"

"There are many Mescalero sub-bands. Also, he is not one to share the secrets of his people. He agreed to assist the Army in campaigns against the Comanche and the Chiricahua Apache, and now the Confederates, but never against the Mescalero. I do believe he has a wife and children among his people, and he does take leave for extended periods to be with them."

"I look forward to meeting this man."

"Please, do not press him about your friend. I need his help. I do not wish to alienate him. I need his help now more than ever."

"I will say nothing to him now, but I cannot promise that I would not someday. Regardless, I will take care. I do not want to interfere with your mission. Let's get the horses unsaddled and staked out for the night."

Things had changed more than a bit since he followed Bushwa Sparks out of the encampment more than a month earlier. His own future was not looking bright at this moment, but he supposed he was better off than

Bushwa who was probably suffering all kinds of torture and deprivation at the hands of his Apache captors. He might even be dead by now. Win could not shake the guilt he felt at letting his friend ride away without a fight. Of course, they would both be dead now.

Chapter 11

BUSHWA AWAKENED AT sunrise with Nascha's naked body pressed comfortably against his own. Most Mescalero women rose well before their men to assure that a fire was burning and something to eat was ready for her mate. Not Nascha. She worked hard but on her own time schedule. He could not complain, because she often offered a morning treat when he awakened.

Danged if he was not about treated out, though. She pouted when he did not claim his husbandly privilege, but he needed a bit of rest now and then. She also tended to be noisy when they coupled, sighing and moaning and occasionally screaming. He never heard such telltale sounds coming from the other lodges, and no other woman had ever behaved this way with him.

All in all, however, he had to admit that his weeks in the rancheria had been more than tolerable. The language was his biggest barrier. Apache conversations seemed to be mostly grunts and tongue rolls, and he had learned no more than a few words of the People's language. Fortunately, Nascha had learned a fair amount of English from her brother Taza, and he had learned that Coyote Chaser had taught her in the past and continued to do so. She was picking up her husband's tongue quickly.

Bushwa had quickly come to realize he had married a very smart woman, probably one who could outthink him most of the time. There were pluses and minuses under such circumstances. Nascha was spooned against him now as he readied to roll out from under the robe. Just as he started to make his move, he felt her fingers dancing on his naked hip. Not this morning. And then his pizzle told him it would be alright. He turned toward her and could make out her sleepy eyes and impish smile as her fingers roamed and she said, "Kiss?"

Her lips touched his and further ignited the fire in his groin. He had taught her about kissing, and she was darn good at it now after the first clumsy, wet attempts. He gathered the Apache generally did not show affection this way.

A voice from outside the wickiup interrupted their morning lovemaking. "Owl Man, you go to Gray Wolf. Him got owl sickness bad. Die maybe." It was Taza.

What in the hell was he supposed to do about it? He was not ready for this. "I will be there. Wait." He could not ask for ten minutes because the Apache did not share such a concept of time.

"I wait."

Bushwa got to his feet and pulled on the soft, white, cotton britches he had taken to wearing along with a buckskin shirt. Then he tugged on the calf-high moccasins that Nascha had fashioned for him. By the time he was ready, Nascha was dressed in a Mexican-style skirt and blouse and in her own moccasins.

"I got to figure something out. How about you come with me?" he said.

"Owl sickness. Ban-jo." She pointed at the banjo resting against the wickiup wall. Then she went to a small stack of her personal things and plucked out a small leather bag. "Maybe this help."

He took it that Nascha was going with him. He was glad about that. Maybe she would help him out of this fix. He had no idea how to cure owl sickness and doubted there was such a thing. He snatched up the banjo and stepped outside into the brisk morning air. A bright sun was creeping over the mountain tops to the east, and it would warm quickly here in the high country.

Taza waited outside, his face a mask of disgust. Bushwa figured that Taza did not approve of late sleepers. He supposed that he and Nascha might be viewed as not carrying their share of the workload. They ate with Taza's family group, but as a di-yin, Bushwa was not expected to hunt or carry out other male chores. Nascha seemed to reign as royalty as well. The band evidently considered her to be the rare woman who might be a di-yin, and she was the wife of a man who was accepted by all but a few skeptics as a genuine di-yin.

Taza said, "You not know Gray Wolf. Wickiup there." He pointed toward the outskirts of the village. "Some not like him. Think he steal. Hits womans hard. Blood comes. Not good. Children, too. Woman must sometimes be hit but not hurt much."

"How did he get the owl sickness?"

"Dark come he go woods and make water. Owl scream and fly over and drop shit on head. Gray Wolf know sickness come."

When they arrived at the cluster of three wickiups, Taza said, "I go now. Bad place to be. Di-yin safe." He turned back to Nascha, who had followed the men, and spoke in Apache. She responded in a harsh tone.

Bushwa suspected Taza had told Nascha to leave also but that she had refused. He was glad of that. Somehow, he felt Nascha had his back covered, something he had never enjoyed with a white woman and admittedly had not deserved. He assumed that his status was fragile here. Like his own people, the Apache would turn quickly on one who did not live up to promise. He feared his reckoning could be forthcoming shortly, and it would be dang hard to grab his horse and make a run for it when he did not even know where he was at.

When Taza disappeared, Nascha pointed to the wickiup opening, signaling that they should enter. He stepped in and found two women on their knees at the side of a man Bushwa guessed to be in his forties. He was covered with a blanket and his face was twisted in agony. The women, one who was on the plump side and near the man's age, and the other slender and much younger, looked up with bewildered expressions. Nascha spoke to them, and they got up and exited the wickiup, seemingly more than happy to do so.

"Wives," Nascha said. "Young one not worry, but first wife like him."

Nascha knelt beside Gray Wolf, who was trembling like leaves in the wind. He looked up at her with mournful eyes. She spoke to him at length, asking questions,

Bushwa guessed. The patient gave short answers. Finally, she got up and spoke to her husband. "Gray Wolf bad man. Good man die and go to underworld. Be happy. Bad man be owl. Do what owl ghost say. He say you help, and he be good man."

"Well, I really don't know what I can do. I ain't been an owl di-yin long."

"I bring medicines I make from plants, yucca root, cactus and others. Some make sick but not kill if not too much. What you call?" She pantomimed a person gagging and vomiting.

"Puking. That's what you are trying to say."

"Puking?" She shrugged. "I find bowl. Put water with medicine, and you help drink. You do banjo now. No weasel song."

Bushwa gathered she wanted something on the calmer side. Maybe a religious song would be good here. He knew most of the words to only one: *Amazing Grace*. Why not take a shot? He positioned his banjo and began picking the strings, trying to find something close to the melody he recalled. Then he began singing, his baritone voice filling the wickiup. A soft voice was not his style, and if it woke the entire village, so be it.

Nascha smiled at him with obvious approval and inspired him. She began scurrying about, finding a small bowl and then pouring a greenish powder from her leather bag into the receptacle and adding water, mixing until it was a thick soup. Then she signaled him to stop.

"What now?"

"You give him this. I tell him he drink and owl sickness go away. I find big bowl for . . . puke. After drink, you do this." She flapped her arms like a big bird's wings.

"Sounds easy enough. How about I hoot, too?"

"Hoot?"

"Yeah. Hoo, hoo," He softly gave his best imitation of an owl.

"Yes. Hoot."

Bushwa took Nascha's potion and let himself down beside Gray Wolf who looked at him with fearful eyes, his body still trembling. Nascha explained to the stricken man that he must drink while Bushwa worked an arm under the Apache's back and helped him sit up. He pressed the bowl to the patient's lips, and the Indian began to drink. He grimaced and tried to push it away, but Nascha scolded him, and he continued drinking.

When Gray Wolf had drunk the last drop, Nascha moved in beside Bushwa and nudged him away, assuming the task of keeping Gray Wolf upright. She placed a large clay bowl beside her. "You fly now. Hoot."

He stood and hovered over the warrior and began to wave his arms, swaying his body like a bird swooping. Then he started his hoots, loud and near deafening in the small space. He was not sure how long he should continue the performance but decided he would wait for his wife's instructions. She had assumed command of this show they were putting on.

Suddenly, the distinctive gagging and coughing of a man vomiting erupted, and Bushwa looked down to see Nascha holding the bowl while the patient spewed vomit. Soon Gray Wolf's reaction eased to dry heaves. Nascha looked up and said, "Stop now."

Bushwa did not protest. He had about reached his limit. He stepped back as his wife helped Gray Wolf move on his side, where he curled up in a fetal position. She was explaining something to the warrior, who, strangely, did not appear to be shaking now.

Finally, she stood and moved to Bushwa's side. "I tell him sickness gone now. You make it fly away and I take what it leave in bowl and put deep in ground."

"We can both do that. Make it look more like a ceremony."

"Ceremony?"

"Don't worry about it. What do we do now?"

"Wait, then take him out of wickiup."

"Take him out. Why?"

"People see you make sickness go."

"Do you really think it's gone?"

"Yes. He think. That make go."

If he understood Nascha right, she was saying that the sickness was in Gray Wolf's head. Damned if she wasn't the cleverest darn woman he'd ever been around.

Fifteen minutes later, they helped Gray Wolf to his feet. The warrior's eyes had cleared, and although he was unsteady on his feet, he did not seem to be suffering any pain, and his earlier symptoms had disappeared. They pushed back the opening flap and stepped outside to find a crowd gathered at the perimeter of the lodging cluster. Bushwa guessed that the entire rancheria was there. A cloak of silence had descended upon all the spectators, and their eyes focused on Gray Wolf, some fearful, others more curious. It occurred to Bushwa that his wife had known a crowd would be gathered and planned this appearance. The woman was a natural showman.

Nascha spoke to Gray Wolf, and the warrior grunted what Bushwa took as a "yes." The Apache spoke in a high-pitched voice to the onlookers. His remarks were brief, but when he finished, the mood of the gathering became relaxed and cheerful, and villagers began to chatter and walk away.

Nascha turned to Bushwa. "Gray Wolf say owl sickness gone, that owl di-yin chase away. What he say of what you do go to all in rancheria. Other bands hear."

"I didn't do nothing except what you told me to do, Nascha. You ought to get the credit. Anyhow, we're partners in this business, and I ain't going to make no bones about that."

"Not know what you say, but like partners. That good—yes?"

"Yes, good, because that's what we are—in everything." He wondered if this is what love felt like, because he was starting to have feelings for this woman that he had never known before.

Chapter 12

May 1862

S EVERAL WEEKS AFTER driving the owl sickness from Gray Wolf's body, Bushwa, known among the Fox sub-band as "Owl Man" now, sat cross-legged in front of the wickiup whittling on a walking stick. He had formed the stick from the branch of an ash tree, one of the few in the pine dominated woods above and below the village. Ash was a hardwood, which made it a special challenge for a knife blade, but it would be a sturdy specimen, and he nearly had the shaft smoothed to his liking. He was starting the last, most difficult step now, the head which would be a replica of an owl with eyes wide open.

Coyote Chaser sat beside him, which was not unusual early afternoon. It was a balmy day with a gentle mountain breeze cancelling the heat sent earthward through a cloudless sky by a bright sun almost directly above. Coyote Chaser said, "I never thought you would have the patience to do something like this."

"You mean the carving? Hell, I been doing this since I was a suckling. Dang good if I say so myself."

"So the head of this stick will have an owl's face?"

"You betcha. Nascha says we can use it in our ceremonies to keep the owl sickness out of the village."

"You listen to Nascha. You are a smart man. She comes to me every day to improve her English."

"I guess I ain't helping her that much."

"She learns much just talking with you, and it seems that the two of you speak more than most Apache couples. My two wives and I do not talk so much, and they have no interest in learning English, since I speak their language."

"It's quiet around here now, almost spooky. Nascha left with the other women to go to the springs for water. Sometimes, I can hear them laughing, so they must be having a good time."

"Yes. Most of the husbands are with the hunting party, and the women don't mind their absence for a spell, especially when we are in the mountain country."

"I wouldn't mind going hunting with the bunch, but Taza didn't ask me."

"Hunting is not expected of you, but you may be welcomed to the hunt when you have been with us longer."

"They think I might make a run for it, don't they?"

"Would you?"

"Time was I'd grab the first chance. Nascha changed that. I couldn't leave her."

"So you expect to spend your life with the Mescalero?"

"Ain't saying that. But I wouldn't leave without Nascha. I figure if I hang on, maybe I can make a deal sometime. Agree to come back sometimes, that sort of thing. And you know, your folks can't always live like this. There is a reservation ahead someday."

"You and I know that. Few of the People accept that truth. I hope I can help them when that happens. With luck, that will be years from now."

"When the War of the Rebellion ends, the Apaches will be first in line for the next war—them and the Comanches," Bushwa said. "Count on it."

"That is my fear. The owl sickness, the coyote sickness and all the other evils lurking out there will be nothing when that happens."

The two friends were interrupted by the sound of a boy yelling from the south end of the encampment. He was racing frantically toward Bushwa and Coyote Chaser, and they got up to meet him. As he drew near, Bushwa judged the youngster to be no more than a dozen years old.

Coyote Chaser said, "It is Nitis. He will be a chief—a peacemaker—someday, if he lives long enough."

The boy was breathing heavily when he reached them and started talking rapidly. He was obviously excited about something, but Bushwa could not understand a word. When the boy finally paused, Coyote Chaser turned to Bushwa. "Nitis watches the north pass. There are well-armed men in the foothills below just starting the trail to the rancheria. He counted at least nine men. He thinks they are scalp hunters."

"Scalp hunters?"

"Some of the Mexican *rancheros* and villages form organizations that pay bounties for Apache scalps. The Mexican government did this some years back but ceased because some Mexican scalps were being turned in for bounties. Identification can be very difficult. These men must have learned that most of the warriors are out with hunting parties right now. They will spare no one, not even babies if they take the rancheria."

Bushwa said, "You go tell the women to take the children and hide. Is the north pass the trail I would have come in on?"

Coyote Chaser thought a moment. "Yes, I think it was."

"Then they are probably an hour away. I am going to grab my Sharps and ammunition. Ask Nitis to take me to a spot overlooking the trail. I will set up and then he can come back and lead whatever men or boys who can help, and we will set up an ambush."

"Nitis speaks English. He understands you. I have an old muzzle loader. It takes a spell between shots, but I will hit my target."

"I can get off eight to ten shots a minute, and my Sharps will take one of them devils out within a quarter mile. How many other men have we got?"

"A few old men who will struggle to get to the trail, three with injuries that kept them off the hunting party. There are three or four boys Nitis's age who can handle a bow well enough."

Bushwa turned to the boy. "Gather up the other boys after you get me positioned. We'll send them bastards home right quick."

Nitis said, "I will do that."

Coyote Chaser said, "You sound a bit overconfident."

"We got two choices, it seems to me: live or die. I ain't about to sit on my ass and wait for some no-good to cut my throat and take my scalp."

Fifteen minutes later, Bushwa was settled in a stone outcropping overlooking the north trail that led to the village. There was room for several others near him, and the remainder could set up on a rise further up to deal with any that got past him. He turned when he heard the rattle of stones behind him and saw Nascha and Nitis, both with bows and quivers of arrows. She moved in beside him.

"What in blazes are you doing here, woman?"

"Partners. I shoot good. Nitis want to be with Owl Man, too."

"Alright, but I got to leave a bit and get folks where they need to be."

She pointed up the slope. "Coyote Chaser in trees. Wait for you."

"I thought maybe he hightailed it out, decided to go chase some coyotes or something."

Nascha scolded him. "Coyote Chaser friend. Good man. Do not say that."

"Yes, ma'am." She had to work some on her sense of humor. Nascha took his words too seriously sometimes.

Coyote Chaser emerged from the trees as Bushwa neared the flat of the plateau. Two wizened, emaciated men followed, carrying spears and knives. He supposed they were no longer strong enough to draw a bowstring, but he did not see them fit for hand-to-hand combat, either. He would give them credit, though, they had answered the call. Soon, two more boys and a limping warrior joined them, all carrying their bows and arrow quivers.

"There are two other warriors who are unable to get up and move about. They are ready with their knives and will not surrender easily if it comes to that."

"Are the women and small children safe?"

"They are going to a large cave with a narrow opening. They will be ready with their weapons, but it would be very difficult for attackers to get to them without death or injury."

"I don't look for that to happen. We will stop the no-goods here. And no quarter. We should kill every last one if we can. We don't want nobody getting away and bringing others back for revenge."

"I understand."

"Well, keep your army in the trees till you hear gun-fire." He nodded toward the rise in the trail. "Get your people on that high ground. Always better to be looking down on the enemy than up. You got to stop any we don't get, but I don't plan on leaving many for you."

Bushwa returned to his post above the trail. Nascha was waiting with news. "Trees cover much trail, but rider show self." She pointed to a rocky clearing about two-thirds of the way up the trail to the village.

It would not be long before they broke into open ground. From that point, their only cover would be to escape into the trees, which would force abandonment of the horses. He must be patient, though, since he did not want anybody to escape back down the trail. They would be moving single file, and he would not fire until the invaders emerged from the cover of the lower trail. He would take down the last man first, his objective being to thwart retreat.

Moments later, a rider mounted on a big bay appeared from the forested canopy and urged his mount onto the rockier, open segment of the trail. Bushwa signaled his companions to stay low, and he hunkered down behind a boulder peering out just enough to keep track of the scalp hunters. The first rider sat erect in the saddle, and was a tall, lanky man with a black beard that dropped over his chest. Bushwa picked him for the leader and guessed him to be a gringo. The first few that followed appeared to be Mexican, but as the riders strung out below, he saw a colored man, and another with several eagle feathers sticking from a black plainsman hat who was likely Indian but not Apache.

They were a solemn bunch, he thought, like butchers readying to slaughter cattle. He worried that the leaders were getting too far up the trail. They must stop some of them here, or they would overrun Coyote Chaser and his defenders. Finally, a rider wearing a sombrero appeared without any apparent followers. Bushwa eased himself onto one knee, aimed and squeezed the trigger. The Sharps sounded like a cannon's roar in the quiet, and the rider screamed and pitched forward before sliding off his mount. Before Bushwa had another cartridge in the breech, Nascha and Nitis were loosing arrows at the approaching riders.

They started to turn around when Bushwa dropped another man attempting to retreat. Panic ruled the trail now, and the leader was screaming at his men to follow him up the slope. Bushwa's Sharps took another man down before the attackers neared and identified their location. "Down," he yelled at his two archers, and he ducked behind the boulder before a barrage of gunfire splintered their rock cover.

He peered out and saw that the scalp hunters were moving on now. Five of the raiders were down, all dead as near as he could tell and two with several arrow shafts protruding from their chests and bellies. By his count there were five left, so Nitis had been one short on his count, not bad considering the distance from his observation perch on the mountainside.

He got off a quick shot before the fleeing scalp hunters disappeared behind a curve in the trail but did not think he made a hit. He turned to Nascha and Nitis. "Stay here. If anybody comes back down this way, kill them."

Nitis must have understood him, because he drew another arrow from his quiver, nodded and grinned and said, "We will be ready."

Bushwa scrambled up the slope above the outcropping. From higher ground he had a view of the hump where the other defenders would slip from the woods. Soon, the scalp hunters appeared on the trail, and the Apaches began to appear, crawling belly down, hopefully out of the line of sight of the surviving raiders. It was a good distance from his vantage point, but Bushwa had no doubt he could do damage with his Sharps. He readied the rifle to fire.

Suddenly, Coyote Chaser jumped up with his muzzle loader in his arms. The weapon exploded, and another attacker fell. Arrows started raining on the scalp hunters, and now they dismounted, two heading for the trees. He aimed and fired the Sharps, stopping the escape of one. A torrent of arrows made a pincushion of the other. One of the old men with his knife clutched in his fingers stumbled over the ridge and headed for the last man standing, the apparent leader.

It was suicide. The attacker fired his pistol at point-blank range sending lead into the decrepit warrior's chest, but he kept on, summoning a reservoir of incredible strength and falling into the scalp hunter, toppling him over backwards, riding the man's body to the rocks, nearly gutting him with the knife blade. There was no need for Bushwa to use his rifle. Both men were unmoving, dead or dying. Silence consumed the battleground now.

Nascha and Nitis joined him now. Nascha said. "We go wickiup now. Nitis come with us."

"But the bodies, we need to do something with them, and the horses need to be collected."

"We go. Coyote Chaser come when dark."

Bushwa did not care if someone else took care of the nasty business, so he did not argue.

Chapter 13

NASCHA AND BUSHWA returned to their wickiup while Nitis went to summon the women and children from their hideaway. Coyote Chaser had assumed command after the battle, and it was clear that any authority grabbed by Bushwa had now ceased. Nitis would tell the women that some would be needed at the battle site and informed a woman named Morning Star that her father had commenced his journey to the other side.

Bushwa downed a nearly full jug of water as he sat on the ground in front of the wickiup. A whiskey bottle would have suited him better. Given the chance, he would be on his way to a good drunk by now. Damn, he missed his spirits more than anything else out in these mountains. In fact, he didn't know if there was much else he missed. If he had stayed with the Reb army, he would still be killing men, and he thought he would rather kill scalp hunters than Yankees.

Nascha stood nearby, gazing at the snow-capped mountain peaks that rose in the northeast. She seemed to be searching for something there, but she did that often, like she was visiting another place, and he had given up asking because she never answered. Following those moments, she tended to become quiet for a spell but would soon change abruptly and return to her usual cheerful self.

Finally, she turned to him. "You do good today. Be war chief. Many die you not here. Nascha thank you."

"Just did what needed to be done. Why didn't you want me to stay to help with the dead?"

"Coyote Chaser not want you to see. Men take scalps. Woman use knives, cut on dead. Take man things, so they not take woman in next life."

"They cut off their balls and pizzles?"

"Yes. I hear you call man things that." She grinned. "Funny. They take scalp hunters into forest for animals and ghosts to eat."

Bushwa decided he did not mind being left out of the celebration. "They did not want Nitis there either."

"Nitis not same as others. Coyote Chaser tell you."

"The old warrior who died—he was very brave. What was his name?"

"I cannot say. We do not speak name of one who dies. They not go to other side, and ghost stay in rancheria or woods—cause troubles."

"I guess I can't say a name if I never knew it, so we will just leave it at that."

Hawk Singing, one of Taza's wives returned to the family wickiup cluster. "I help Hawk Singing now. Onawa first wife and go to punish scalp hunters."

"Hawk Singing misses out on the fun, huh?" He guessed Nascha understood, because she gave him a look of disgust and went to help Hawk Singing prepare a meal.

At dusk, after a good meal, Bushwa figured he would snooze a bit, but just as he started to enter the wickiup, Coyote Chaser appeared. "Well, old friend, I was told you might be paying a visit. I don't suppose you brung a bottle of some good booze with you—or plain old rotgut would do."

"No, it is the Apache curse, worse than any of the evil ghosts that lurk in the darkness. It is the curse of many whites as well, although few are wise enough to know it."

"Count me as one of them whites. I ain't looking to be wise if I can't have a good drink now and then. Come on in anyhow. We can talk inside. Nascha's helping with the old man that got hisself kilt. He was a brave one, but I guess we don't say his name no more."

They stepped inside the wickiup and sat down in the near darkness. Coyote Chaser said, "Nascha has informed you about not speaking the name of the dead."

"Yeah, but I never knew his name in the first place."

"Many Apache believe that speaking the name of the deceased delays the spirit from its journey to the other side. That means his or her ghost may wander about and even cause mischief."

"So will they bury him someplace?"

"That is one Apache way. A small cave or crevice in a canyon wall is preferred—covered with stones, of course, to discourage predators. Digging a hole in the ground is a last resort. Only family and a few close friends will help—no white man's ceremonial funeral unless a great chief has died. They cannot wait for the return of his son, but the son's wife will prepare the body with painting of his face and see him wrapped in a blanket. Her mother-in-law—the dead warrior's wife—must not participate. This man who is leaving us will be revered for his brave act and it will hasten his arrival in the underworld. He has an old horse that will be taken to the burial place and killed nearby and left for this journey or buried with him if possible. Any clothes or possessions not buried with the deceased will be burned along with his wickiup to discourage return of his ghost."

"You are getting me nervous with all this talk."

"You must learn about these things. Your status will soar as high as the eagle flies after your actions on this day. I wish you would permit me to start teaching you to speak the language of the People. It would increase your power even more."

"Don't want to learn Apache beyond the words I pick up now and then. I never been to school and ain't going to start now."

"Very well. You have earned a place among the Mescalero without my help. Just know that I will support you however I can. I am not unselfish. I know it is to my advantage to be the friend of a man like you."

"Don't know nobody back where I come from that would say that, and I am dang grateful for your guidance."

"Before I go to my wickiup, one piece of advice. Listen always to Nascha and become Nitis's friend. That is what his name means in Apache—friend. The good spirits call to Nascha and Nitis in ways that they do to no others. Your destinies are intertwined. Nascha has said as much to me."

"You and my wife talk about these things?"

"She shares thoughts when I teach her English, only because the coyote knows much more than any creatures about the spirits' plans. Sadly, the coyote will only reveal such things to me in his own time."

"I might just as soon not know about them dang plans, but I'd sure like to know more about this kid."

"His father is known as Bodaway. He is a scout for the bluecoat soldiers. He will not help with war against his own people, but he has fought the Comanche and now continues in this war between the two white tribes. He knows many important people among the whites and can speak English sufficiently to act as interpreter if necessary. I teach Nitis and his younger brother and sister English at his insistence, and Nitis can read and write the language. He has a brilliant mind, and for that he is shunned by some of the boys his age."

"I didn't talk to him much, but he spoke a few words, and I thought he understood what I was saying just fine."

"He did, I assure you. Nascha insists that Nitis is a treasure who must be protected for the People. Visions have told her this."

"I don't believe in visions, but I could make up a few if it would help my owl chasing work."

Coyote Chaser sighed. "I do not recommend it."

Too late, Bushwa thought. It was time for him to come up with a vision, "What about this Bodaway? How often does he come here?"

"He will be in the rancheria a few weeks at a time every two or three months. He brings many important supplies on packhorses when he visits. He purchases these with his wages and shares with the People. He appears to move easily between the whites and the People. And he will be informed that he is not to speak with you."

"Why not?"

"You know the answer to that question."

Obviously, he was still a prisoner. He was apparently free to do as he pleased so long as he did not attempt to escape to the white world. Well, he was a patient man, and he sure wasn't suffering any. He was having more fun than he had experienced in a long spell. And with the damn war going on, where was he going to escape to? No, he would bide his time, but he would sure like to know what became of young Win Evans.

Chapter 14

WIN AND RENATA spent two days and three nights in the canyon preparing the site as their hideout. They constructed a lean-to shelter with tree limbs and brush, stretching the canvas tarp over the top to ward off rain. Win was dubious about the need for the canvas roof since he had yet to witness a drop of rain in this desert country, but Renata insisted that it did rain on occasion and that spring storms could be merciless.

They also constructed a crude gate across the narrow canyon entrance that would permit them to turn the horses loose and give them free run when they were camped here. A stone fire ring for cooking added a domestic touch to the campsite. The third night was the first that they shared the shelter. Win found that he could not

Ron Schwab

be oblivious to the fact he had a stunning woman rolled up in blankets and sleeping within an arm's reach away.

Renata did nothing to encourage his fantasies, and he tried to keep a healthy distance. Fortunately, she could not read his mind. Or could she?

The morning of the third day, Renata announced, "We must go to the Rough and Ready Station. I have a message for Bodaway. He will be waiting there, wondering why I am late. He will carry it to the Mexican Springs Station more than a two days' ride from there. Another courier will take it on to Tucson and deliver it to the military contact."

"Well, I can finish breakfast cleanup while you round up your mare. Buddy will come when I whistle. What are the chances of trouble at the station?"

"The station manager, Butch Zimmer, is pro-Union. He is an important link and was with the Army officer who recruited me. His life is already at risk for his work."

"But what if they identified him, and he turned on you to save his own skin?"

"Not Butch."

"I am just saying we cannot be too careful."

Her eyes flashed anger but quickly calmed. "Two men tried to kill me. You don't think I am being careful?"

"I would like to know more about the links in your chain of information. We should talk about that."

"You were a Confederate soldier. How do I know you aren't looking to save your hide?"

"You don't. But it is unlikely I would have killed a fellow soldier if I had not made my choice."

"I shouldn't have said that. Sometimes I have a quick temper. I apologize."

"Accepted. Now let's get moving."

An hour later, astride their horses, they were back in the foothills overlooking the desolate lands west of the Rio Grande. They had strapped bedrolls to their saddles, deciding they would likely spend the night near the stage station.

"It will take us most of the day to get to Rough and Ready," Renata said. "They've got lodging at the station but no separate rooms for men and women. One double bed with a bundling board down the middle for privacy. I used to stay over when I made this run myself. It is a good day's ride from Las Cruces. I made the first weekly run, but then Charlie Hopkins started acting as courier from my place to the station. He claimed it was too dangerous for a woman. It's not any worse for a woman than a man, but I didn't resist the change."

They dismounted so their horses could drink from a stream that fed into the Rio Grande. "You never mentioned Hopkins before. Who is he?"

"He is a tavern owner from Mesilla. He checked with me weekly to see if I had any messages. If I did, he would get them to Bodaway."

"So he had direct contact with you and could swear to your spying activities?"

"Well, I guess so, yes. But Charlie is solid Union. He has been with me from the beginning, collecting information about Confederate activities. A saloon in the middle of an enemy-held town is a perfect source."

"I wouldn't argue with that. My concern is that he could change your message between here and the Rough and Ready Station. And then you are relying on what he is telling you for part of your information."

"I have other sources." She was silent for a moment. "You are not a very trusting man, are you?"

"Let's just say I'm careful. I picked up a few things from my friend Bushwa. Now, how do we get to this Butterfield Station?"

"We need to pick up the stagecoach trail. That would be due north of here. From there, you just follow the trail west to the Rough and Ready. We will pass through some rugged country, several canyons and gaps between

mountains at some points, but the trail itself is not difficult. It just threads its way between all the obstacles."

"Well, let's ride then. Time is wasting."

Chapter 15

Renata still did not know what to make of Winston Evans. He had been a good worker at the livery and followed
instructions unquestioningly and to the letter, although
if he spotted a task that needed doing, he promptly went
ahead and tended to it without waiting to be told. But she
sensed now that she was not in charge anymore and she
was uncomfortable with that notion.

Still, she knew that she needed Win. The reality was
that she could no longer deal with this situation alone.
She would try to relax the reins for now but would not
hesitate to give them a yank if he turned the wrong direction.

The riders reached the Butterfield Trail sooner than
expected and reined their mounts west, moving slowly
and side by side for a spell. "Not much of a trail," Win
observed.

"It's not traveled as much as it was before the rebels took control of this part of the territory. The stagecoach mostly brings mail, and there is less of that because of inspection points to the east. Soldiers sift through the mail and open anything suspicious. Everybody knows this, of course, and would not be attempting to send messages related to the war effort."

"I can see why there would not be many passengers these days."

"All one way. There are some leaving to escape to Union territory. I'm surprised that Butterfield didn't just close this run when control of this area changed hands."

"A business doesn't make a dollar if it's not operating. If they can take some losses for a spell, they will be better off in the long run. Starting up costs a lot. Besides, I am not a brilliant general, but I don't see how the rebels are going to hold this area for long. They are isolated from support and supplies here. It would take months to call in more troops, and they can confiscate horses and supplies to a certain point, but those will dry up. We saw that with our cavalry regiment. We were being converted to infantry because of horse losses and not enough replacements. What we had left were divided among the other regiments."

"You were cavalry? You never said before."

"Yep. A volunteer. I was a corporal when we took our leave. Bushwa was twice a sergeant, but I outranked him at the time. Not that it mattered to Bushwa. He wasn't impressed by rank. That and a tendency to brawl when he drank too much made his promotions temporary."

"And this man was your friend?"

"Real friends overlook the flaws in each other sometimes. That's why they stay friends. Bushwa would have laid his life down for me. In fact, he might have done just that."

"What do you mean?"

Win told her about the encounter with the Mescalero and Bushwa's trading himself for his freedom.

Renata listened in near disbelief. "And his weapon was a banjo?"

"Yep. Bushwa has a knack for finding strange ways out of trouble. You know, sometimes I worry that he is dead, but the truth is he is more likely to be chief of a tribe. I just hope I find out someday. One of these days, after I learn more about this country out here, I will go looking for him. I can't go on with whatever life I've got left without knowing."

"I've never known anyone quite like you, Win. You are a hard one to figure out." She nudged her mare ahead and quickened the pace.

Less than an hour later, the trail began to wind through narrow deep-cut ravines and gorges with steep sides that loomed above the riders. They were not far from mountain foothills closing in on each side, and Renata knew that they would encounter areas like this during their journey and then the flat, open desert would suddenly appear again for a good stretch. The landscape was ever-changing in this part of New Mexico Territory.

Win sidled Buddy closer to her mare and signaled her to stop. She slowed the pace and reined in her mount. "What's the matter?" Renata asked.

"Dust cloud ahead. Horses coming our way. It could be anybody. Apache. Confederate cavalry. I don't think we want to meet up."

She supposed that made sense. "What do you suggest?"

"There are breaks in the wall at different places. We should take the first one that gets us out of sight. If we have time and can hide the horses, I would like to see if we can get up high enough to see who the riders are." He gestured to the right. "There appears to be a break just ahead. Let's check that first. I don't know how much time we've got. Sometimes, you can see dust for several miles in this desert country, but it could only be minutes away, too."

They rode ahead, Win slipping into the lead. He reined his blood bay into the crack and disappeared, and Renata followed. Luck was with them. They dismounted and led the horses up a sandy and rocky slope where the base of the wall leveled off into the desert. It was a short climb over a gradual incline to reach the summit above the wall that would afford a view of the riders. After staking the horses they scaled the stone surface.

"Flatten out," Win said when they were nearly to the top. "We don't want to risk being seen if they are the wrong people."

She could see the dust whirlwind at the far western edge of the gorge now. Three riders emerged from the dust behind seven or eight horses that the riders were obviously herding to some destination. As they neared, she recognized Charlie Hopkins's distinctive calico mount and the sombrero that always topped Charlie's head. She started to rise, but Win's firm hand pinned her shoulder to the rock.

She looked at him, her brown eyes smoldering with anger. "Let go of me. It's Charlie. We need to talk."

He did not release her. "Look again."

The riders were nearly below them now, and her heart missed a beat. No, it could not be. Fanned out off to each side of Charlie Hopkins were two men wearing Confederate gray. She froze and said nothing more until they headed easterly toward Mesilla on the Butterfield Trail. Win had released his grip on her shoulder with the riders' passing, and she sat up now and looked at him.

"Charlie was riding with Confederate soldiers, and he did not appear to be a prisoner," she said.

"No, he seemed to be the leader."

"He is a turncoat."

"So am I, of course. Maybe Charlie has been with the Rebs from the beginning. He has probably just been doing his job like you have. My dad always said most things are a matter of perspective. It's not always easy to tell right from wrong or truth from fact. It depends on whose eyes you are looking through. He always reminded me to be slow to judge. That doesn't mean we don't make judgments eventually."

"You are too young to be making philosophical pronouncements."

He grinned. "We need to find a watering hole for the horses and get up the trail to the Rough and Ready."

It was darn hard to stay mad at this guy. He was an expert at weaseling out of a fuss.

Chapter 16

I T WAS MIDAFTERNOON when Win and Renata sighted the Rough and Ready Station. He reined Buddy in, and Renata looked at him quizzically. Win said, "Let's ride over to that hillock behind the station and get a better view of the place before we ride in."

"Do you think something is wrong there?"

"I don't know, but I am wondering where your friend Charlie picked up his little horse herd."

"You are thinking the horses came from here?"

"I am just curious."

They headed their mounts off the trail and veered away from the station for a short distance before angling toward a dune-like knoll that erupted from the desert no more than fifty yards from the station. They left the horses at the base of the hillock and made their way to the top.

"Nothing moving down there," Renata said, pulling her hat brim lower on her forehead to shield her eyes from the sun's glare.

The stagecoach relay was not an impressive operation, Win thought, but he supposed it was all Butterfield needed for a change of horses. The facilities consisted of a rectangular adobe building with what appeared to be a small stable attached. Outside the stable was a small horse corral, empty except for a lonely mule. Two goats seemed to be finding something to graze on some distance from the station, but he could not imagine what. There would be nothing to support a horse for more than a few days within a mile from the place. He supposed that someone was hauling in hay for the critters from someplace, an added expense for the business.

He wondered how a business could make a profit maintaining little stations like this spread across the west. He had always been interested in how money flows worked. He had learned a lot about such things—what the educated called economics—from a friend who could barely read or write. But Bushwa Sparks understood how numbers worked and what a business had to do to make a profit. He had early on decided that Bushwa could teach him more than some Harvard professor who had never operated a business in his life.

"I wish we had brought a spyglass," Win said. "Do you have one at the house?"

"Yes. My father's."

"I will see if I can pick it up when I go back into town."

"You are planning to go to town?"

"We need to check in at your mother's, and I don't think you should be anywhere near there right now. Besides, I want to visit a saloon in Mesilla."

"You are making no sense."

"What is the name of Charlie Hopkins's saloon?"

"The Yellow Rose. Why? Wait—no, you can't go there."

"I gather Hopkins hails from Texas. Sounds like a good place to learn a few things. We will talk about it later. For now, I think it is time to make our visit to the station. You follow me about ten horse lengths back. Be ready to grab that rifle if somebody starts firing. That's not too likely. I think any unwelcome visitors have been here and gone." Seeing the perturbed look on her face, he added, "Please."

They led their horses toward the front of the station, thinking it would be best not to be mounted if gunfire erupted and they were forced to seek cover. Win noted that there were two windows at the front of the building, both partway open. The door was closed. He stopped some fifty feet from the door and waited for Renata to come up beside him.

"Shall I call for Butch?" Renata asked.

"Yeah. We can't stand here till sundown."

"Butch, Butch," she hollered, "it's Renata."

After a few minutes, the door opened, a dark, lean man wearing a sombrero stepped out with a rifle cradled in his arms.

"Bodaway," she said, and handed the mare's reins to Win and raced toward the man. She slowed when she reached him but still greeted him with a quick hug, although the man remained unemotional, surrendering only a small smile as he eyed Win suspiciously.

Win led the horses ahead and hitched them to the weathered rail that he would not have trusted for less docile mounts. Renata waved to him to join her and her friend.

"Win, this is Bodaway. I have told you about him."

Win stepped forward and offered his hand, which the man accepted with a quick grip. "I have heard good things about you." This was the Mescalero Renata had spoken of. Wearing the sombrero, the man could have passed for Mexican. Maybe that was the idea. Win decided that he determined racial background more by attire than anything else in the Southwest given the dominance of mixed bloods. He had heard that many Mexicans were more Indian than Spanish if you sorted out the makeup of the melting pot.

Renata said, "Bodaway, where is Butch?"

"He sleeps inside. He lives, but he was bad beat when I find him almost where you stand. Nose break, but I fix. Eyes swell shut. Head cut."

Renata brushed past him and headed for the door. "I've got to see for myself."

The Apache shrugged and looked at Win. "My horse in stable, but others not here when I come."

"We saw them being herded east on the stagecoach trail. Two Confederates and a man named Charlie Hopkins. I assume they gave Butch Zimmer the beating. I don't know why."

"Hopkins." Bodaway nodded his head as if not surprised.

"Why don't we go inside and see what Renata has planned?"

"Renata smart woman. Sometimes, trust too much."

Win wondered if the Indian was including him among those she trusted too much. When he entered the station, Win saw Renata sitting next to a cot pushed up against the east wall. On it lay a white-haired man with a brushy mustache, his face bloodied and bruised so badly, it was difficult to identify any other features. Renata was bathing his face with a wet rag she had evidently dipped in a nearby water bucket. Both eyes were so swollen, it was difficult to tell if the man was awake or sleeping. A strip of cloth was also tied about his head, probably to cover the cut Bodaway had mentioned.

Win's eyes swept the room, which was quite large. It was Spartanly furnished with four straight back chairs scattered about and an iron heating stove in the center of the room and a small fireplace for Dutch oven and kettle cooking. What in blazes did you find to burn in a stove or fireplace out in the middle of nowhere?

The wall opposite the bed had shelves stacked with supplies, and there were boxes lining the other wall with more. He supposed that what was not sold to travelers was appropriated by the relay manager for survival. It would be a challenge to get supplies to this place, though. More expenses.

"Win and Bodaway, come over here. Butch wants to talk." Renata said.

Win and the Apache joined her. Win guessed that Butch had awakened, but all he could see were slits for eyes.

"I got to tell you what happened," the old man croaked. "I couldn't make no sense of it when Charlie showed up here with a couple of Johnny Rebs. They was looking for

Ren and thought I should know her whereabouts. Beat the shit out of me trying to get me to say. I would've died before I said, but I didn't know anyhow."

Renata said, "But he took the horses."

"Said the station is closed. The bastards are closing the Butterfield line till after the war. Charlie's a damn traitor, and I thought he was a friend. I need to get word to the bosses about this before another stage comes through. Hard telling what happens if it does. The Rebs will stop it for sure if it gets close to Mesilla or Las Cruces. Don't know where I go. Guess I stay here till somebody kills me. I got supplies for a few weeks. They left me my mule and wagon, and I can kill a rabbit now and then, maybe a deer if I go into the foothills."

Renata said, "Win and I will stay with you for a few days until you decide what's best and you feel well enough to travel someplace. You aren't going to be left alone till you are well enough to decide."

"You are a good woman, Ren, but I've got to tell the company."

She looked up at Bodaway. "Can you still make the ride to Mexican Springs?"

"Yes, I do that."

"Wait till morning. I need to make the Army aware of the problem here and that my messages may have been flawed. I can send a separate letter to the relay manager there about the closing of the Rough and Ready Station."

Win had to sort this out. He did not like the idea of staying at the station, but he could not think of an alternative. Renata was back in charge for now.

Chapter 17

AFTER THREE NIGHTS at the Rough and Ready Station, Win was ready to move on. He was nervous about the prospect of Confederate soldiers dropping by to confirm that the place had been vacated, and he was ready to get on with the mission, although the immediate objective was obscure to him.

He had spent three nights sharing a bed with Renata in the station's guest room. The bed was divided by a removable bundling board providing a vertical barrier about two feet high to separate two sleepers. Still, it was a strange feeling. Fortunately, he was so tired he had little difficulty sleeping.

He would have preferred to sleep in the stable, but Renata had insisted they should be at the same location in case of attack. The building was a veritable fortress with a thick oak door and inner shutters for the windows, all secured by steel latches at night. The risk of a stealthy, surprise entry by intruders was slight.

Win still lay in the bed of the small L-shaped room, which was squeezed into the shorter arm of the L. The room's other contents were in the stem which afforded semi-privacy in one corner. He was waiting for Renata to finish dressing in that spot where there was also a chamber pot. It had somehow become his responsibility for emptying the contents every morning. There were no furnishings beyond a few chairs and a wooden bench upon which they could fold and place their clothes. Renata seemed less concerned about modesty than he did, but he turned his head away as she emerged from the corner covered only by the shirttails of a loose-fitting shirt to snatch up her britches from the bench. He assumed there were undergarments of some kind underneath, but he could not help imagining there were not.

She paused for a moment, slipping long legs into her denim britches as she spoke. "As soon as I get my boots on, I will get a small fire going in the fireplace. I guess it is biscuits again unless you want beans."

"No, thanks. I'll do the biscuits if you don't mind getting the fire going. Are we leaving today?"

"You can look at me now. It feels strange talking to the back of your head."

He rolled over and faced her and saw that she was seated in a chair now tugging her boots on. "Trying to respect your privacy."

She laughed. "What privacy? It is best not to fret too much about that the way we're living these days, but I will give you credit for being more considerate than most men I have encountered. But to answer your question, yes, I think it is time to pull out. We are probably pressing our luck by staying here, and Butch is getting around well enough now. He insists he is staying. I told him we would get more supplies to him as soon as we could, but he's not concerned."

"He is a tough old varmint," Win said. "Are you still okay with returning to our canyon hideout?"

"Yes, I think it's the safest place to headquarter. Bodaway will find us there. He should have delivered the letters to Mexican Springs by now and be on his way to visit his Mescalero band at their rancheria across the Mexican border. He said he would not be there more than four or five days and then would head back. If we have an emergency message to get to Cottonwood Springs, you said you could do it."

"Sounds easy enough. All I would have to do is follow the Butterfield Trail and take an extra horse."

"You are getting deeper into Apache country there. That's my big worry."

"Apache swing up this way, too, and I don't think Confederates are roaming further west."

"I still don't like your idea of visiting The Yellow Rose."

"But you want to confirm troop numbers and movements. Hopkins has probably been feeding you false information."

"I'm sure that's the case, and I think you are right. I had just as well tell you. This so-called spy chain of mine consists of no more than five people—four now, I guess, with Charlie Hopkins out of the picture, and I'm not as confident about trusting everybody."

She did not seem to be in a hurry to leave, and he was ready to get up. A visit outside to water the sand would become urgent soon. He swung his legs over the side of the bed and wearing nothing but his baggy, cotton undershorts walked over to the bench to retrieve his own shirt and trousers. He had not bathed since leaving the canyon and his clothes hadn't been washed for days either. He stank, and here he was sharing a room and bed with a beautiful woman. A hell of a thing.

There was no water well at the station, and the place was dependent on roof run-off into a stone cistern on the rare occasions rain visited and whatever could be hauled from a spring at the base of the mountains several miles distant. Butch Zimmer lived out a brutal existence but did not seem to be an unhappy man. There were lessons there someplace.

"Don't worry," Renata said. "I don't smell so good either."

"How did you know what I was thinking?"

She chuckled. "I saw you sniffing your shirt."

His face flushed with embarrassment. "I didn't know I did that."

"We'll get cleaned up before you satisfy my next request."

He looked at her with suspicion as he slipped into his shirt and commenced buttoning it. "I am listening."

"How would you like to visit a bordello while you are in Mesilla?"

Win thought if his face was not red before, it would have to be now. She had an impish smile on her face, and he could tell she was enjoying his discomfiture. She was almost playful this morning, a side of Renata Rutledge he had not seen before. "That's kind of a personal question, ma'am, but I have never found it necessary to pay for such pleasures."

"Bragging?"

"Just saying."

"Well, the reason I asked the question is that I have an important informant at Mary's Manor in Mesilla, one of the more respectable of such . . . uh . . . accommodations. It caters to the higher-class patrons—prosperous businessmen and military officers, for instance. Mary is the proprietress and madam, but more importantly, staunchly pro-Union. She has eight girls, and all feed her information they collect from military customers. She is a very successful entrepreneur and takes enormous risks through her involvement. I dare not be seen there, and she must be informed about Charlie Hopkins, who, fortunately, has not been her contact. Until now, she has always communicated directly with me."

He was uneasy about visiting the bordello but could see how such a contact could be critical. "Yeah, I guess I could do that."

"I will give you instructions before you visit. There is a password that you must give Mary before she would speak with you freely. I assure you that your virtue will be safe with Mary. She has no interest in men beyond the money her girls harvest from the fools."

The statement made him curious about Mary, but her preferences when it came to men or women had nothing to do with his mission. "We will have plenty of time to talk about all this. Right now, I need to finish dressing and then look after the horses."

Renata took the hint and stood up to leave the room. "I have got chores, too, if we want to get an early start. By the time you finish in the stable, I will have things ready for the biscuit maker."

Chapter 18

BUSHWA AND NASCHA walked a good mile south of the rancheria to a lonely pine rooted on a naked stone ridge with most of its higher limbs charred by a lightning bolt. Nascha had insisted that the tree's bare, blackened branches were a favorite roosting place for owls at night. They would not catch sight of any owls early afternoon, but she hoped for a harvest of feathers from beneath the tree. She also wanted one of the blackened branches from the tree.

As they approached, Bushwa said, "This was a dang rough walk and then we got to make it back again. I don't see how owl feathers can be worth it. And a charred branch?"

"Big medicine. Put two feathers on skunk hat. Show people you no afraid of owls."

"They should know that. I'm Owl Man, ain't I?"

"Must always show. Owl Man big di-yin now. Must show people that still have powers always. Not afraid of owl feathers. Powers still with you. I put feathers in hair, too. Strong powers in our wickiup. Make am-u-let from wood. You do things with blade. You do this maybe. Fight lightning sickness."

"Now that's a sickness I ain't heard about yet. Is there anything your people don't get sick from?"

"Coyote Chaser say lightning is arrow of Thunder People, carry sickness if hit tree and smell smoke. Lightning sickness like owl sickness. Food come up. Water come from what you call 'ass.' Get weak and maybe die if di-yin not come. Fox band does not have lightning di-yin. Maybe am-u-lets help."

"Don't know where you got that word, but maybe we could make some money selling them amulets. I could carve some good stuff—animals maybe if we can think of one that don't carry sick spirits."

"Trade maybe. But must honor spirits. Know you not believe. But honor because People believe always. Belief why you live."

She had a point. Sometimes, he wondered how much of this stuff Nascha believed. It did not matter, he guessed. And it was likely a good thing that she respected the religion of the Mescalero. Who was he to say they were not right? Regardless, as Nascha pointed out, he would not be alive if not for his supposed ability to deal with owl spirits.

"Whatever you say, sweetheart. You ain't steered me wrong yet. I will honor the spirits."

"Sweetheart?"

"Something a white man says sometimes to his woman. Shows he cares for her."

She beamed. "You like Nascha?"

"I sure do. I like you lots. You are my woman. The only one I want." For now, anyway, he thought.

"Get no other woman for wickiup?"

"Never." He was sincere in that statement. He could barely service the one he had. Two would kill him. Besides, he wasn't sure he could do anything while the other was watching. No, Nascha would be his woman while he was with the Apache, and he was starting to accept that he would not be leaving anytime soon.

Nascha was right. They found almost a dozen feathers scattered in the vicinity of the tree, some weathered but others fresh specimens. She placed them carefully in her little rawhide bag and smiled with satisfaction.

Bushwa said, "How did you know owls roosted here?"

"This spirit place. Spirits bring me here nights before I be your woman. See and hear owls many times here.

Never afraid. Owls friends. Tell me Owl Man come soon. Then you come."

Suddenly, he wanted her in the worst way. His desire was so overpowering, he did not understand it. "I want you," he said, his voice husky.

She smiled. "I know. Spirits say we make child here." She was already pulling the Mexican blouse over her head and revealing her generous breasts.

Bushwa wasted no time joining her.

Chapter 19

S EVERAL DAYS AFTER his visit to the owl tree with Nascha, Bushwa saw a man he assumed was an Apache walking with Nitis toward the woods below the rancheria. The boy was talking animatedly with the man, and Bushwa thought it strange because he rarely saw an Apache male strolling with a younger boy. Stranger yet, a sombrero perched on the man's head, and aside from moccasins he wore Anglo attire.

He saw Coyote Chaser sitting outside his wickiup and walked over to his friend's family cluster and sat down beside him. "I seen Nitis walking with a man that had a sombrero atop his head. Ain't seen the feller around here that I recollect."

"The man is his father, Bodaway."

"He's the man that works for the Yankees."

"Yes, and it would be wise for you to stay away from him. Taza has told him not to speak with you."

"It sounds like Taza don't trust me."

"He trusts you as an owl di-yin. He wants you to be one of the People, but you have not earned your place yet."

"He thought my taking on the scalp hunters was the act of a chief. That's what he said."

"The band is grateful for your leadership that day, but that does not make you Mescalero."

"I can't change my blood."

"Mescalero is more than blood."

"I ain't going no place, but I got a friend that was with me the night I went with Taza. I was to meet up with him in Las Cruces. I just want to know he is alright."

"What is his name?"

"Win Evans. He is a young feller, not much more than a kid."

"I will speak with Bodaway and ask him to listen for that name, but he will have other duties and cannot carry on a search."

"Well, I guess I got to settle for that right now. Can I send a message with Bodaway in case Win turns up?"

"No."

Bushwa decided he was pressing his luck and got up, thinking he would give Nitis a little more of his time when the boy next came by. He had been hanging around the wickiup like a stray dog lately. Maybe it was time to scratch that hound's ears a mite.

When he returned to his own wickiup, he saw Nascha standing outside, her eyes fixed on the northern horizon. He looked in that direction but saw nothing unusual. He stepped up beside her. "You look worried, sweetheart. What do you see out there?"

"Thunder People come. Lightning. Much rain. Rivers soon no hold water come from mountains."

"I don't see nothing. Sky looks clear blue. No trace of a cloud."

"I tell Taza. People must hide red horses and all red things. Not ride spotted ponies. Eat no food till storm go."

"I'm sorry, sweetheart, none of this makes sense. Why not eat?"

"Make thunder arrows hit. Eat when thunder lose teeth."

"I see." But, of course, he did not. He decided not to ask about red horses and what he took to be pintos but would accompany her to see Taza and get permission to hide his dapple gray. He wasn't sure if the white spots on the gray counted or not. And maybe they were okay so long as they were not being ridden. This was more confusing than all the dang rules the government put out.

He could sense the panic in the rancheria that evening when black, menacing thunder clouds approached, displaying flashing bolts of lightning in their midst. When thunder roared, Nascha informed him that the Thunder People were shouting. When the first light drops of rain splattered on the ground, they took refuge in their wickiup and sat on the buffalo robe side by side, waiting for the storm to strike.

In minutes a raging thunderstorm struck the mountain village, rain pouring from the sky. Thunder sounded like the roars of cannons, shaking their little lodge, and lightning delivered flashes that illuminated the entire rancheria. In the background, Bushwa could hear the crying of small children and the moaning and chanting of adults.

Nascha snuggled up against him, sharing a blanket she had snatched up to ward off the sudden chill. "Thunder People not send arrows to us. Thunder Child protect."

He turned his head toward her. "And who in blazes is Thunder Child?"

"Baby we make under lightning tree."

"That has only been a few days. You can't know that you are going to have a baby."

"I know."

And she probably did, he figured. What if she was right? He had never fathered a child before. Well, none that he knew about anyhow. He knew what caused babies, but a man never thought about that with a willing, naked woman by his side. He had damned well better be thinking about it now.

Chapter 20

WIN WAS GLAD to be back at their canyon campsite. It seemed like the nearest thing he had to home these days. Even the horses liked it here and were impatient to get to grass and water as he unsaddled the two mounts. Renata did not appear to share their delight. She had gone quiet on him during the journey back, but it did not especially worry him because his own mind was on the mission to Mesilla.

The sun was several hours from disappearing over the canyon rim, and he had told Renata he would tend to the horses and get a fire started if she wanted to bathe at the small water pool beneath the spring. She brightened noticeably but looked at him warily.

He had assured her, "I will keep a good distance and turn my eyes away. You have some cover from the willow stand over there, too. Your mother put a fresh bar of lye soap on my bed while I was packing, unless you've got your own."

"No, I was not thinking about such things at that time. Leave it to Madre to think of it."

He had retrieved the soap and handed her the bar while she dug out her only remaining clean garments from her haversack and immediately headed for the pool. He decided to give her a bit more time and set about gathering up some more wood. Day temperatures were starting to heat up, but nights still turned chilly, especially as a person ventured into the mountains.

He figured to fix a decent supper tonight. He was starving, having to settle for jerky and hardtack at noon. Butch had given him a can of peaches and several slices of ham as a parting gift, and he had the other ingredients to make ham and beans and a Dutch oven cobbler. After his mother died, his father had surrendered most cooking duties to the son, and, of course, Bushwa only cooked if he could not get out of it. Win found that he rather enjoyed the chore, and Renata did not fight to take over the task, although he thought she could be a bit more helpful when it came time for cleanup.

When he returned to the campsite, Renata already had a fire going and was sitting next to it, combing wet, shoulder-length hair that had a reddish tint to it in the sun. She was a beautiful creature, he thought, convinced that he was not lowering his standards because of a fe-male famine.

"Feel better?" Win asked.

"I do. Much better. I didn't take long because the water is ice cold. It's not the kind a person is inclined to soak in. Now, if I can just get my hair dry before sunset. Go ahead with your bath if you like."

"I got supper planned out, but I don't dally in cold wa-ter either, so I think I will do just that while I've got some warm sun to help dry me off."

He returned to the campsite wearing a clean shirt. His dusty britches would stay on duty for now, but he liked the feel of clean undershorts and socks. He had others at the bed and board in Las Cruces and figured he could re-trieve extras there, perhaps change before visiting the sa-loon and bordello. When he reached the firepit encircled with stones, he found Renata sleeping, head drooping forward and chin resting on her chest. He did not disturb her and set about preparing supper.

Renata woke with a start when the Dutch oven's lid clanged as he was putting it in place to commence baking the cobbler. "Oh, I dropped off to sleep and didn't know you were back."

"That's alright. You are tired. Catch a little shuteye when it can be caught. That's what Bushwa would say."

"But you have got to be tired, too."

"I plan to be in my bedroll early this evening. I am going to stake the horses out near the shelter tonight. Buddy lets you know if guests of any kind show up. He is about like a watchdog."

Later, as dusk triggered a rapid cooling in the canyon and Win and Renata had eaten all they could handle, they sat at the fire with steaming cups of coffee in their hands. Renata said, "This is nice. It seems like years since I have had a meal like this."

"Everything tastes better when you have been starving."

"I suppose. But this was a pleasure."

"It is tomorrow's breakfast, too, assuming you want to move ahead with your spy mission."

"It would be nice to have a few days of leisure here in the canyon, but I need to work fast to set things right. Troops are on their way from California to retake what the Rebels have claimed. They will need good information. I am hoping Madre has a report on Fort Bliss and El Paso. An old Army officer delivers that, usually stays a night or two, so he can claim to be Madre's suitor. Colonel

Baker is probably seventy years old and looks older, but he is smart, fearless and tougher than he looks."

"I should go to your mother's house first. I might want to change clothes and pick up a few things. If she has a message from the colonel, I should rendezvous with you before I go into Mesilla. In case things don't work out there, you would at least have his information."

Her brow furrowed, and she looked at him. "I don't like to hear you say that 'in case things don't work out.'"

"We know that is a possibility. I have my eyes open. This is dangerous business. One slip up, and it's over. The only consolation is that if they learned I am a deserter, I would face a firing squad anyhow. You are in danger, too."

"I know that, but you got drug into this by circumstances."

"I still had a choice to hightail it out. They would never have caught me. But I thought about this and feel I am doing what I should be, that I am a part of something bigger than me. I can say this and still respect the men I fought beside for a short time."Renata said, "I'm glad you told me that. I have been feeling guilty for getting you involved. I haven't figured you out yet, Winston Evans, but I have never met anyone quite like you. What do you think is going to happen with this war?"

"I don't know what is going on back east, but my sense is that the Confederates are swatting mosquitoes out in this part of the country. They hit one and another shows up. I did learn this much, and you should pass it on. They have no reliable supply lines, they are short of horses, and their ranks are thinning by the day. I am no general, but I think if they get hit hard at a few places, their forces will collapse, and they will be on the run. I heard they have visions of taking Colorado and moving west and eventually capturing California. They plain don't have enough men or weapons to do this. And they have got to feed the men they have got. This has not been thought out. It is somebody's delusion."

"You have thought about this a lot, haven't you?"

"Yeah, it has been on my mind. And about tomorrow. I think I should show up at your mother's place in the afternoon, leave my horse at the livery and take my rifle and saddlebags into the house just like I planned to be an overnight guest. If somebody is keeping an eye on the place, he would be more suspicious if I showed up at night. This would also give me daylight to see if I can identify someone who might be watching."

"That makes sense, but what do I do in the meantime? I can't stay here if you intend to contact me with any information from Colonel Baker before you make your other stops."

"I must come back across the Rio Grande to go to Mesilla anyhow. You wait someplace on the west side of the river to meet up with me. I will give you any message from Baker before I make the Mesilla contact. It will be late, but I will return to that spot after my Mesilla business, and we will ride on a ways and try to find a place to lay out the bedrolls. At that hour, I don't think we want to travel the rugged route back to the campsite."

"My head is spinning, but I don't have a better idea."

Win got to his feet. "I am going to bring the horses in and then we can grab some sleep."

"And I will clean up for a change. You have been spoiling me, and I haven't minded, but partners at least share the work."

Win liked the sound of that word: partners.

Chapter 21

THE RIO GRANDE had changed markedly since their last crossing a week or so earlier. The gentle flow had been replaced by more turbulent waters rising a good two feet higher between the banks. Win and Renata stood not far from the west bank's edge, surveying the crossing they had made a week earlier.

"I don't like this," Renata said. "Spring thaw of mountain snows from the north and west have started. It will get worse before it gets better over the next few weeks. I have never seen the Rio Grande go out of its banks here, but it does some places. Do you think you can cross?"

"We should be alright. I am a good swimmer if I need to free up Buddy. I have swum in worse waters back home and along the Mississippi."

"I can swim, but I am not the best."

"You won't need to be crossing anyhow. You insisted that you watch me cross. When I am on the other side, you head back to the hideaway we liked near the foothills."

Renata said, "I've been thinking. Don't waste time coming here with word from Colonel Baker. Go directly to Mesilla and get your work done there. And please don't follow through on your plans to visit Charlie Hopkins. There's too much risk, and I am going to be worried sick. I don't like it either that you will be crossing back over the river when it's dark to get to Mesilla."

"At least, after I am finished with business there, I won't need to cross the river again and can go directly to the hideaway. You go on ahead and wait for me there. It can't be more than an hour from Mesilla even with the dark slowing me some."

"I suppose not. I just wish I could go with you."

"We have been through that. We can't risk someone seeing you and recognizing you. Odds are that the house is being watched at least part of the time, and you would not dare go to Charlie Hopkins's saloon with me. If he happens to be there, it's all over for both of us."

"I just told you not to go there."

"I'll see how things look when I get to Mesilla."

She sighed. "You've got a stubborn side." She reached over, clutched his hand and squeezed it. "This isn't worth your life. Don't do anything foolish."

"Me? Heck, lady, that's my middle name—Foolish, or I wouldn't have teamed up with Bushwa Sparks back in Jefferson, Texas."

"That's not very reassuring."

"I'll be fine." He released her hand and headed for the riverbank. "If you will excuse me, I will be shedding my clothes for the crossing." He sat down and pulled off his boots and socks before standing and stripping down to nakedness. He did not look toward Renata, figuring she could turn her head away or not. He had more important things to deal with. He rolled up his shirt and britches as tightly as he could and stuffed them in his deerskin bag along with the boots. He anchored the bag to the saddle-bags with rawhide strips, positioning it on Buddy's rump and hoping it would stay above the water most of the journey.

He placed his gun belt and Colt in the saddle bags and left the rifle in its saddle scabbard. He would do a weapons' check at Martina's house. He looked back at Renata, who evidently had not turned her head away, and gave her a little wave. She responded with a feeble wave.

He led his horse down the gently sloping bank to the water's edge and waded into the water which had turned ice-cold since his previous crossing. Soon, he stood waist-high in the water that was trying to lift him from his footing and push him downstream. Buddy was not resisting, and he was confident the horse would follow now that they were a third of the distance across the channel. He released the reins and commenced swimming.

Midstream, the current was winning, pushing him downstream. He gave less resistance, knowing he would lose that battle, and let it carry him some as his strokes took him ever nearer the east riverbank. They were quickly free from the worst of it albeit a good half mile downstream when he and his horse gained footing again. He grabbed Buddy's reins and led the blood bay to a widening place in the river where the bank was not so steep, and they made their way to high ground with relative ease.

Now, they would need to head back upstream to assure Renata that he and Buddy had made the crossing. She likely feared that the river had carried them away and drowned them. First, he retrieved his clothes from the bag. A naked man might attract too much attention if he encountered others on this side. He was pleased to find that the garments were not drenched, a few wet spots here and there but quite tolerable.

While slipping into his undershorts, he glanced across the river and saw Renata waving enthusiastically. She had followed them downstream. He waved back and hollered, "We are fine. Nice swim. Now get out of here."

"You are insane," she yelled back. "I am going now." She mounted her mare and disappeared before he finished dressing.

It was nearly four o'clock when he arrived at Rutledge Livery & Mules. The front stable door was open but no stable hand in sight. He supposed Martina had been unable to find help to cover all the hours. He put Buddy in a stall, brushed him down, forked him some hay and fed him a bit of grain before he took his gear and went to the house.

He knocked on the door, not wishing to frighten Martina by walking in unannounced. He could hear movement in the house, but she did not come to the door immediately. Win suspected she was peering between curtains someplace to identify the visitor. When the door opened, she stepped back for him to enter. When the door was closed behind him, she grabbed him so tight she almost knocked him off his feet.

"Oh, my Win," she squealed. "Welcome home, my son. Welcome." She pulled his head down and smothered him with kisses. "I am so happy you are here. I have been so worried." Then she stopped abruptly and released him from her embrace. "But Renata . . . she is not with you. Is she—"

"Renata is fine, Martina. We agreed that it was not safe for her to come here, but there is work to be done in Mesilla, and I told her I would tend to it. I will meet her across the river later tonight, and we will go to our safe place."

"Then you cannot stay the night?"

"Not this time. But I need to get a change of clothes in my room and clean up some."

"A hot bath. I will put water on the cookstove and start it boiling if you will pump some water and fill the tub partway after you find the clothes you want."

"Well, I just had a river bath, but it was more mud than water. Renata will be jealous. Of course, I will just get all muddy again when I go back across the river to Mesilla."

"There is a big ferry there now, my nephew Carlos told me, to connect the towns. You will need to go north along the riverside from Las Cruces. You will find it. The ferry will carry both you and the horse for two dollars. It is too costly for many people. Of course, the Confederate soldiers do not pay. Their Army constructed the ferry. A soldier will be operating it. I suppose that is a concern."

"It is worth a try. The river is flooding some, so I don't know if it would be in use, but I will sure try to catch a ride."

"You will stay for supper?"

"Yes, I can stay that long, but I must be gone before seven o'clock."

"Oh, and I have a message from the colonel to send with you. He said it was very, very important when he was here two days ago."

"Renata was hoping you would have something from him."

"His message is sealed, and he did not discuss it, but he seemed rather excited about the contents—in a happy way. Usually, he is downcast and pessimistic about the war."

"I hope to collect some good news tonight, but it is better that you not know about it in case you are interrogated. Has anyone been here yet?"

"One man. A young well-uniformed gentleman, who was very polite. He asked if he might visit with Renata. I told him she had gone to El Paso to search for mares to mate with our jacks for breeding mules and that I did not know when she might return. I invited him in for a mug of coffee, and he surprised me by accepting. I suppose he was looking for signs of Renata."

"That was a bit risky, wasn't it?"

"Oh, I think not. He seemed a very nice person. He told me he hailed from Mississippi, which I had guessed from his beautiful accent. He said he had graduated from West Point and that his father was a lawyer. They did not own slaves, he had been quick to mention. I am sure he is torn by this war. The good people are not all on one side, are they?"

"No. Not the bad ones either."

"Anyway, he was here but a short time, and he may return again. He did take a stroll through the stable before he rode off. Looking for two horses, perhaps?"

"Very possible."

Chapter 22

AFTER HIS PLEASANT visit to Martina's boarding house, Win retrieved Buddy and rode on toward Mesilla, following the east bank of the Rio Grande. In the darkness, he could not confirm with certainty, but it appeared the river had risen another foot, maybe two. He hoped horse and rider would not be forced to enter the water again.

He was attired now in a brown coat and string tie, which Martina had appropriated from her husband's closet along with the white shirt that had replaced his own. Martina had noticed that he was about the same size as her husband and suggested he would look less suspicious if he dressed like a businessman on a mission.

"But I need a mission," Win had said.

"You have horses for sale at a ranch over twenty miles from here. You are going to Fort Fillmore in the morning to speak with the commandant there."

"Of course, the Rebels are desperate for horses. The story makes perfect sense. You are a natural spy. Maybe the Yankees have the wrong Rutledge working for them."

"I do not recommend that you tell Renata that."

"I assure you I will not."

He saw the ferry bobbing in the water along the east riverbank ahead. Thankfully, it was on the near side. He reined his mount into the cover of a cluster of young cottonwood trees and paused and waited for a spell, his eyes searching the trail behind him. He had done this several times on his journey from the boarding house and had picked up no sign that he was being followed. Either the boarding house was not being watched or he had not been judged a suspicious visitor. Of course, a single watcher would have been forced to desert his post to follow a stranger, so it would not be difficult for a man to persuade himself that he should stay put.

He headed Buddy forward, and as they approached the ferryboat, he caught sight of a man sitting on the ground, his back leaning against a thick post that appeared to support a heavy rope that stretched across the river to another post on the opposite side. A big, unsaddled horse was staked nearby. Several rope lines extended to the ferry from the big rope and were anchored at each end of the raft-like ferryboat. The river end of the ferry also had another rope stretching across the river to the shadowy figure of another man leaning against the post on the west bank.

Win dismounted and led Buddy up to the man whose chin was lowered and resting on his chest. The only sign that he was a soldier was the gray Confederate cap resting on his head. He was a beefy, black-bearded man, and his snores were the only sound in the remote area of the landing.

"Sir?" Win said, awakening the man with a start.

The soldier's eyes popped open, and he looked up at Win with frightened eyes before he relaxed, probably, Win thought, because he recognized that his visitor was not an officer.

"Yeah, what do you want?" the stocky man said, scrambling clumsily to his feet.

"Is the ferry operating tonight?"

"That's what I'm here for. One more ride to the other side, so I can stable the horse, get me some grub, and head for the barracks—well, maybe a drink or two before I go there." He winked and grinned.

"Well, I would be your last ride, the horse and me, if the price is right."

The soldier hesitated and looked Win over. "Four dollars?"

The coat and tie were going to cost him. The soldier intended to make a little profit for himself. "I don't know. I would go three."

"Well, I been here for twelve hours and so has Oscar across the river. Four dollars would be mighty kind."

"Oscar gets a share?"

"You betcha. We come from the same county back in west Louisiana. I wouldn't cut him out."

Win figured he would buy some cooperation from the man. He would not likely ask so many questions if they remained friendly. "Well, considering the state of the river and your long day, I'll go four dollars."

"Do you got gold?"

"I do." He dug four coins from his money pouch and handed him the money.

"Not that I don't trust the Confederate paper, but it ain't all that welcome around here."

"I suppose not."

Fifteen minutes later, they were headed across the Rio Grande. The ferry was sturdy and large enough to hold ten horses with riders, and more weight might have stabilized the craft more in the turbulent water, Win supposed. On the other hand, since oars were not useful in this water, it was no doubt an easier pull for Oscar and his horse to tow them by the long rope from the other side. He understood now that the cable-like rope overhead kept the current from whipping the ferry about in the water. It was a simple system, and he had seen others like it in Jefferson. Someone with experience designed it.

The occupants had to yell at each other to converse because of the river's roar, but he decided to risk a question or two. "You are a mite overworked it seems," Win said, "with a twelve-hour shift."

"Damn right we are. But troops here are spread thin. They've sent half the garrison up north to help take Santa Fe. They got men deserting like rats on a sinking ship up there, I guess. Short of horses and food, but what they take north from here leaves us even shorter." He hesitated. "You ain't no soldier, and you ain't South. What's your business here?"

Win was glad for Martina's backstory. "I am a rancher, and I've got horses to sell. I don't care who buys them if they can come up with gold coin. I will be going to Fort Fillmore in the morning to see if I can make a deal."

The soldier nodded. "Good timing, I'd say. They pay us with paper, but I'm guessing they got gold money set aside for when they need it. Of course, the army might just decide to help themselves to them horses."

"They are a good distance from here, and I won't tell them where even if they kill me."

"You ain't so dumb. Well, unless you end up dead."

Chapter 23

WHEN WIN SAW the mass of men roaming the dusty streets of Mesilla, he decided to switch the order of his visits. The Yellow Rose saloon appeared to be overflowing, and he was uneasy about the way several men eyed his horse. He did not like the odds of having Buddy stolen along with all his gear and the food Martina had sent with him. Under no circumstances would he hitch the horse outside the saloon or anywhere else along this section of the street. He would not be helping the cause if he were left afoot.

He nudged the gelding down the street away from the crowds and toward the dead-end Renata had told him about. The end of the street took him to a large adobe church—Saint Paul's, according to a sign framed by adobe brick off to one side of the entrance stairway—Catholic, he assumed, the dominant religion of the territory.

Win had been raised and baptized Methodist but had not visited a church since meeting up with Bushwa some five years back. He supposed he would find his way back someday but did not dwell on it.

The dead-end was essentially the top of a tee, where the traveler must choose to turn right or left. He chose left, welcoming the quiet hillside area he was riding into. He had suddenly entered what appeared to be a residential area if it were not for the signs in front of the five houses that formed a cul-de-sac and rose on the gentle slope of a hillside above the street. There were horses tied to hitching posts here and there, and he saw two men entering one of the houses, but there was no one outside milling about.

The properties were all well-maintained, and he gathered that this was the neighborhood of upper-class bordellos where the price of a poke might be significantly more than the single dollar establishments Bushwa always claimed was his limit. Two of the adobe houses had the appearance of Spanish haciendas, but the one that drew him was a frame plantation-style structure at the furthest end. He rode toward that one, and as he neared, saw the sign that read "Mary's Manor."

There were two hitching rails out front that would easily hold a dozen horses, although there were presently only three mounts tied there. He felt much less concerned about horse thieves here and dismounted and hitched Buddy onto the rail. He removed his rifle from the scabbard, however, and carried it with him up the half dozen stone steps that led to the manor's yard and from there took the brick walk that led to the front door of the house which was set back almost fifty feet.

There was a metal door rapper shaped like a deer's head adjacent to the ornate door and he rapped several times. Soon the door opened, and a pretty blonde woman peered out, her eyes perusing him before she spoke. "May I help you, sir?"

"I am here to see Mary."

"Why don't you step inside?"

He stepped in and she closed the door. "My name is Sarah," she said. "Mary is not seeing anyone. I am presently available. So are Monique and Pilar." She nodded toward two women seated on a settee in the room which might have been the elegant parlor of a mansion. One was decidedly of Spanish heritage, the other, a dusky dark-eyed woman reminded him of an octoroon he had met once in New Orleans. All the women who presently shared the room with him were quite beautiful and alluring and exuded class that the uninitiated would not have expected to encounter here.

"I am hopeful Mary will see me," he said. "Please tell her that George Washington is here to speak with her."

"George Washington? Well, I guess I can inform her, but don't be disappointed if she can't see you. She is a very busy lady."

"I understand."

She seated him in a padded, leather-covered armchair directly across from the two prostitutes. At least, he assumed they were prostitutes. He squirmed in his chair and feared that he was blushing as they eyed him and smiled. The dusky lady, bent over to brush something off her shoe, revealing more than ample breasts beneath the low-cut gown. He felt that he was being seduced by their eyes, and the discomfort in his trousers confirmed it.

Shortly, Sarah rescued him. "Mary says she will see you. Follow me."

Sarah led him down a carpeted hallway and stopped at a closed door. "This is Mary's office. She is expecting you. Just go on in. If you need something else when you are finished, whoever is acting as hostess at the front door will be glad to help you."

He had never visited a bordello before, but under different circumstances he was not certain he could have resisted the temptation. He wondered what the prices were at an establishment like this. He sighed and opened the door to the madame's office.

When he entered the room, he was struck by its businesslike appearance. The office was nice, but the furnishings were simple and not pretentious, including a huge desk behind which sat an attractive young woman wearing wire-rimmed spectacles and a white, high-necked blouse nearly hidden by a navy-blue jacket. The wall behind the desk was lined with bookcases filled with books.

Parchment sheets were spread out on the desktop, and the woman gathered them up and pushed the papers to the side of the desk before she stood, stepped around the desk, and extended her hand. "Mister Washington, a pleasure to meet you, sir." She shook his hand with a strong grip. Releasing his hand, she gestured to one of the chairs in front of the desk. "Please be seated and tell me how I might be of assistance."

Win was not certain how to open the conversation, but she had made the first move his. "Well, ma'am, I am a friend of Renata Rutledge's."

Mary's brow furrowed and she removed her spectacles. "The Union spy? The Confederates are looking for her, you know."

He was baffled by her response. She almost sounded pro-Confederate. "She is my friend."

She smiled. "I am teasing, Mister Washington. But word is out that Ren is a fugitive. I take it she is safe."

"She is for now, anyhow. And you may call me Win."

"That is short for something."

"Winston."

"And I am Mary. It is best that we forego using last names. Of course, I use mine only on legal papers anyway."

"I am here to collect any information you have collected regarding the movements of Rebel troops and the strength of their force in Mesilla and Fort Fillmore."

"I have kept a daily record of information collected by my ladies and myself since I last passed a message on to Ren. Just a moment." She got up from her high-backed chair and walked to a desert landscape painting hanging on a side wall and removed it to reveal a safe imbedded in the wall. It took her no more than a few minutes to open it and remove a large envelope. She closed the safe and returned the painting to its place.

Returning to her chair, she shoved the envelope across the desktop to Win. "I will give you a summary. The officers at the local garrison are on the verge of panic. Most of the troops have been reassigned to the north. There are between 150 and two hundred men available to defend this so-called Confederate territory capital. They can't count on reinforcements from Fort Bliss and any other support is likely months away, maybe never if the war back east does not go well for the Rebels. Of course, the Union would need to find their own troops to move them out."

"That's true enough, but this information will be valuable in the hands of the right people. You are taking a big risk to perform a critical service to the Union."

"I have a personal stake. Since the Rebels moved in, our business has been hurting. We have been forced to reduce prices. Their army has not paid its soldiers for months, and many pay in Confederate dollars, which many businesses are not accepting, or if they do, the value is discounted by half. Some nights my ladies are entertaining fewer than half the usual customers. I have other investments, and I will not sell those to keep The Manor open. I have acquired some nice real estate holdings, but they would sell for very little while the Confederates control the territory. I can hold out for three months. If I do not see Union troops taking back Mesilla in that time, I will be locking the doors."

Win concluded that he had encountered a very astute businesswoman. He guessed her to be no more than twenty-five years old and wondered how such a young woman could be so successful in so brief a time. Were whorehouses truly that profitable?

"Well," Win said, "I had best be moving on. I have another stop to make. I wonder if I might leave my horse hitched out front for a spell longer?"

"Of course, but may I ask where you are heading?"

"The Yellow Rose. I thought I might see if I can pick up information from the drinkers there, chat with the owner a spell."

"Not Charlie Hopkins. Stay clear of him. I have a page in the envelope about him. He is working for the Confederates."

"We just learned about that a few days ago. I guess I can talk about it now. He was a courier for Renata."

"He is also one of our patrons. Sarah is his favorite, and he often shows up here half drunk. She is my best at cajoling information from a randy male. He bragged that he had worked his way into the Union spy chain and was feeding false information. What I have given you is very important. I suggest you not take a chance of running into trouble at The Yellow Rose."

"You have verified everything else I've learned. I think I will take your advice. I should really get back to Renata anyhow."

She pushed her chair back and stood, clearly dismissing him. "I will let you be on your way now. I will continue to learn what I can. Feel free to visit anytime—for business or pleasure." She offered a mischievous smile.

Chapter 24

BUSHWA KEPT HIS eyes on the Apache called Bodaway during his visit to the Mescalero rancheria. He was disappointed when he saw the warrior ride out of the village on the morning of the fourth day. He had understood that the periodic visits sometimes lasted several weeks and hoped that he might be able to catch Bodaway alone and send a message to someone in Las Cruces concerning his whereabouts. Of course, he had no clue regarding the potential recipient of such a message. Well, maybe next time. By then, his captors might loosen the reins a bit and give him more opportunity to talk to Bodaway.

In the meantime, he would continue to make the best of his situation. He was not a man to make himself miserable about something he could not control, and truth be known, he was a long way from being willing to part with Nascha. That woman had a hold on him like no female ever had.

He stood outside the wickiup this morning, having eaten breakfast of pieces of roasted rabbit and a cornbread that seemed to be mostly crust. Some blackberry jam would have made the meal more tolerable. A cup of coffee would be welcome right now, he thought.

He had taken up a few notches on his belt since joining the Mescalero, but the weight loss was not voluntary. Food was his biggest deprivation in his life among the Apache. Sometimes there was very little to eat, except for a few dogs or an aging horse roasted over rancheria fires. Neither might have been so bad if he had not known what he was eating. Bread and biscuits rarely made with flour were nothing he would ever crave here. Even the occasional rustled beef did not taste the same.

On the other hand, he had not eaten much better during the last month of his Confederate army days. He longed for a heaping plate of hot cakes doused in maple syrup along with a platter of bacon and fried eggs topped with a few steaming cups of black coffee. He vowed that someday, somehow, he would eat a civilized meal again.

Nascha had joined other woman on a trip to the stream to collect water in the crocks. She would be a spell, because he had learned that group water collection was a social event among the women where they sometimes bathed and always exchanged gossip. In some ways, he had observed, all folks had things in common. He missed Nascha's presence when she was gone for even a short while but looked forward to hearing any news when she returned.

He saw Coyote Chaser walking his way, a somber look on his face. That likely meant nothing since he had never seen his friend laugh or even crack a smile. He rarely showed up for a casual conversation, however, so Bushwa assumed he carried a message of some import.

"Good morning, Coyote Chaser. It is a beautiful day, ain't it? Nary a cloud in the sky, a nice breeze drifting down over the mountaintops."

"I bring a message that I fear will bring storm clouds to your day."

"The council voted to kill me or something?" He spoke the words with no concern about that possibility.

"No, but your life is in danger."

"You know how to catch a feller's attention. I'm listening."

"There is a warrior who challenges your authority as a di-yin. He claims that you are a fraud."

"Well, ain't nothing what says he's got to believe."

"He wants to prove your weakness by death combat."

"I gather he ain't talking about playing poker. What's this feller got in his head?"

"You will each choose a weapon and face each other in a circle of chiefs. This is not a game. Warriors may be present also but no women. This will take place just before sundown in two moons."

"You mean day after tomorrow?"

"Yes."

"What if I don't want to be a part of this silly crap?"

"Your prestige will suffer. Others will begin to doubt. Your life may depend upon your continued acceptance of the people as a di-yin."

"Ain't I already proved myself—dealing with the owl sickness, fighting off them scalp hunters?"

"Taza came to me about this after a meeting of the four chiefs. They have approved of the combat. He asks me to tell you because he feels awkward with your language."

"Well, who is this dang challenger anyhow?"

"His name is 'Kuruk,' which means 'bear.' He is the biggest of all the warriors in the rancheria."

"I seen him around. Always got a scowl on his ugly face and wears a half dozen bear claws around his neck. Looks like he gets more than his share at the trough."

"Yes. That would be the warrior. I am to report to Taza. Will you fight him? He has chosen a knife as his weapon. You must select yours."

"Well, hell, I'll just use my Army Colt and end it quick-like."

"No, no. It must be a weapon that is used for hand-to-hand combat."

"Can I use a hatchet?"

"Yes, that would be accepted."

"No, wait. I think I will use a war club. I got me one from the feller that had the owl sickness. I like the feel of that in my hand. Lighter and faster than a hatchet. Yeah, I'll fight the son-of-a-bitch."

"I will inform Taza."

"You do that, and I will tell Nascha about this little party." Bushwa's guts roiled thinking about the confrontation with Kuruk. He preferred his duels to be with guns, and the thought of a blade in his belly gave him the shivers. If he could, he would hightail it out of the village. Since that was not an option, he hoped Nascha would come up with a plan—like slipping some poison in Kuruk's water before the fight.

Later, when Nascha returned to the wickiup, he told her about his dilemma. "I can more than hold my own hand-to-hand using my fists. I ain't so sure when the other feller is swiping a knife blade at me."

"We talk when rancheria sleep. I know then what we do. Nitis help."

"How in blazes does Nitis get involved in this?"

"Want to be di-yin helper. Be di-yin for peace maybe. I need him for this."

"I got to get to know that kid better."

"He like you be friend."

It had occurred to him previously that he could possibly reach Nitis's father through the son. Nothing to lose. "If I live through this, I will be the kid's friend."

"You live. Nascha not let you die."

That mollified him for a spell, but as dusk faded into the black of night, he became increasingly nervous and edgy. Danged if he wouldn't take his chances and make a run for it if not for Nascha. The mere thought of leaving her behind devastated him. It occurred to him then that this must be what love is. He had never felt like this about anyone or anything before with the exception, perhaps, of his old gelding Star, dead for more than five years now.

Nascha disappeared for a short time after dark, and when she returned, she smiled at him and nodded. He had no notion what that meant, but he had learned not to press. She would explain when she was ready. Finally, when the village quieted and the two were settling in for the night, Nascha motioned for him to sit down with her on the bed robes. He hoped she did not have lovemaking in mind, because his pizzle was no more than a limp worm this night.

"I put little bag outside Kuruk wickiup. Two owl feathers."

"You gave up two owl feathers to that oaf?"

"Warn him owl ghosts watch. One feather next dark time."

"You don't think that is going to scare him off?"

"No, but not like. Worry him, I think."

She was trying to make Kuruk nervous, shake his confidence. Not a bad idea, he thought, but it wouldn't change the odds that much. "Can't hurt none, I guess."

"When go fight Kuruk, take ban-jo. Do weasel song and give owl prayer."

"I don't know an owl prayer."

"Make one. Most not understand but Coyote Chaser tell others. Taza, too. You stay away from Kuruk knife, but when owl hoot, you hit."

"And what if the dang owl don't hoot?"

"Owl hoot. Now you mate with me." She began slipping out of her cotton blouse and dress.

Ron Schwab

He took off the moccasins that he was starting to pre-fer over boots. She was already helping with his shirt. "Nascha, I don't know about this. My pizzle ain't working so good tonight. I think he needs a night's rest. Maybe wait till after I fight Kuruk."

"Pizzle work for Nascha."

And pizzle did. The woman could perform miracles, and he hoped she came up with one two nights from now.

Chapter 25

FLAMES DANCED FROM the fire in the center of the circle, lighting the combat area and casting a glow on the somber faces of the chiefs and warriors gathered to observe. Bushwa stood just outside the fire ring with Nitis at his side holding the banjo. Kuruk stood on the opposite side, unlike Bushwa having stripped off his shirt and displaying chest and arms sheathed with muscle.

Bushwa figured that revealing his own torso and shoulders would not intimidate and had not removed a stitch, not even the skunk skin cap. Kuruk glowered at Bushwa, and his lips were twisted in a contemptuous sneer. Bushwa tried to appear calm and bored, a look inconsistent with his churning guts.

Three beats on a drum signaled that the fight should begin. Kuruk stepped into the circle with his hand

Ron Schwab

clutched to a hunting knife that Bushwa guessed to be Mexican in origin. Nitis handed Bushwa the banjo, and he joined Kuruk in the ring. He commenced plucking at the strings and was soon rendering his loudest version of *Pop Goes the Weasel*. Kuruk froze and looked at him dumbfounded while he sang.

When he was finished, Nitis reached out and took the banjo and then stepped back. Now Bushwa raised his hands to the sky. He could hear the low mumbling of his audience, impatient and confused. Kuruk still made no move in his direction.

Bushwa began to speak. "Oh, great Owl spirit. I call upon you tonight and ask for your protection. There are them foolish men that doubt I am your di-yin. A man has challenged me to fight till death. I do not want to kill him. Protect me, but don't let him die on my account. You brought me here to help these people, not to kill them. Thanks for listening to your servant, old mighty Owl."

Nitis broke through the circle, the banjo secured in one arm, and presented Bushwa with his war club, a big chunk of smoothed granite bound to a carved handle just short of two feet long. Bushwa accepted the weapon, and Nitis immediately disappeared into the blackness of the night. Bushwa knew—or hoped—the boy would still have the battle within sight so he could perform his task.

Kuruk was moving slowly toward him now like a mountain lion stalking prey. Bushwa took a few steps toward his opponent, trying to ward off any notion that he feared the man. He was taken by surprise when the warrior suddenly lunged forward and drove the knife toward his midsection. He ducked away but not before he felt the searing pain of the blade slicing flesh along the side of his ribcage.

The Apache stumbled past him, got his footing and swung around to attack again when horrified screams erupted from the heart of the wickiup clusters. Kuruk stopped instantly, giving Bushwa a chance to regroup. Some of the Mescalero in the circle got to their feet and several headed toward their wickiups, but Kuruk turned back to business. Before he took a second step toward Bushwa, however, the distinct, sharp "hoo-hoo-hoo" of an owl sounding an alarm rose from the forest beyond the rancheria, then a softer response from what seemed to be another owl.

Kuruk turned his head toward the sound for just a few seconds but long enough for Bushwa to drive the stone head of the warclub into the side of the warrior's skull. The knife flew from his hand, and he dropped to the earth like lead. Bushwa looked around. Fewer than a third of the onlookers remained, and they were starting to move on, all except Taza and Coyote Chaser, who were walking toward him, their faces impassive, neither revealing how they felt about the outcome.

Taza passed him by and knelt beside the fallen Kuruk. Coyote Chaser paused and nodded approvingly. "There will be no more challenges to your powers as owl di-yin. A few may suspect your assistance from Nitis and Nascha, but they would not risk questioning your powers. An owl could not better Nascha's imitation of its own cry."

Taza got up. "Kuruk lives. No woman to help, but we take to lodge. Tell sister. She maybe help."

Coyote Chaser said, "He will live just like you prayed to the Owl spirit. This will cause you to be respected even more by the People." Then he looked at Bushwa's bloody fingers that were pressed against his left side. "You were wounded, I will help you back to your wickiup. Nascha can care for the cut."

"I might need a little steadying. My shirt is soaking up blood."

"Can you walk to your wickiup?" Taza asked.

"I should be alright," Bushwa said, before he collapsed on the ground only a few feet from Kuruk.

Chapter 26

BUSHWA SMELLED SMOKE before his eyes opened and he realized he was stretched out on the buffalo robe in their wickiup. He was shirtless, but a blanket had been tossed over him, and he could feel the warmth of the fire nearby. His ribs ached, and his fingers went to the soreness covered with cloth, what he guessed to be a poultice of some kind.

He turned his head and saw Nascha and Nitis sitting next to him, their eyes fixed on the patient. Nitis grinned broadly and Nascha gave the loving smile that always warmed him. "Guess I didn't go to hell anyhow?"

"What is hell?" Nascha said.

"Ain't going to try to explain that now." A sharp pain ripped through his left side, and he moaned.

Nascha said, "Hurt three, maybe four, sunrises. I sew and put plant medicines on. Nitis help me. He good boy."

Bushwa blinked, trying to clear the fog in his brain, but the haze and dizziness remained. "Thanks, Nitis. You did good tonight. It is still tonight, ain't it?"

"Yes. Village quiet because of Owl fear, but most not sleep." She pressed a clay jug to his lips. "Must drink. Water good medicine now."

He lifted himself up on his elbows while she held the jug to his lips. He would have preferred a whiskey bottle, but water had never tasted so good. He was not ready to quit drinking when she pulled the jug back.

"Wait," she said. "More soon."

Nitis said, "I must go, Owl Man. My mother will worry. She knows I am here, but she does not approve."

"She don't like me, I suppose."

"It is not a matter of like or dislike. She fears that I am becoming a white man. She thinks my father brought a disease back from his adventures with the whites."

"I'm guessing you speak American better than I do. Maybe she's right. You sound like a dang professor, or worse yet, some law wrangler."

"What is a law wrangler?"

"Lawyer. Do you know what that is?"

"Yes, of course. I have read about lawyers. That is what I would be. I can help my people when the time comes."

"Lord help us."

Bushwa

"Coyote Chaser is my teacher. My father wanted me to learn English and asked Coyote Chaser to help. He has taught me to read and write. My father has brought me six books back now. I have read them many times, but I keep them hidden. Others might not approve."

"Coyote Chaser told me I should ask you to teach me the ways of the whites. I have many questions, especially about the Bible."

Bushwa found himself flattered at the notion of being a teacher and liked the idea of an audience for his tall tales. He was not so sure about the Bible since he had never read the Good Book. He had been to church a few times, though. He figured he knew enough to talk his way around the subject. He supposed he was closer to Christian than anything else.

He said, "Son, you are welcome here anytime. I will be glad to learn you about the ways of the white world." What he didn't know, he could make up.

After Nitis departed, Nascha said, "Nitis be mighty di-yin when the peace comes. Many of us dead then. Others no longer free, but he help Apache then. Nascha think Great Spirit sends you here to teach and help Nitis."

He did not like her talking about death and the future. Now was enough for him. Too many folks wasted time thinking about the next day or month or year ahead when tomorrow might never be. Grab the pleasures of the here and now was his creed. Deal with today's troubles. That made for better living as far as he was concerned.

He felt suddenly sleepy, and his eyes started to close.

"Water, then sleep," Nascha said. She placed a firm hand against his upper back and helped him sit up.

"Yes, ma'am." He drank his fill and was nearly asleep before he lay back into the robe and blankets.

Chapter 27

THE RAIN HAD started several hours before Win and Renata returned to the canyon from the visits to Las Cruces and Mesilla. They were drenched by the time they reached the canyon campsite. After unsaddling the mounts and dropping the saddles and supplies at the canvas-covered shelter, they led the horses deeper into the canyon to the shelter offered by a cluster of cottonwoods. The spot also offered a nice stand of mixed grasses for the animals.

They had not staked the horses, confident that that the mounts were compatible, and that Buddy would not stray far from Win. The gate across the narrow canyon entrance would deter them if they wandered that far. When the horses were settled, Win clutched Renata's hand and led her, slipping and sliding, back to the camp.

Thankfully, the canvas kept the shelter dry even as sheets of rain began falling from the sky. They shed their wet clothes down to undergarments, abandoning any modesty now, crowded by the food and gear, and moved their bedrolls to the center of the shelter till they overlapped a bit before crawling into their blankets.

They had spoken little since meeting up again. Because of lightning flashes in the north sky, they had decided not to stay at the hideaway and to head back to their shelter in the canyon. Finding and negotiating the trail to the canyon had been the priority, and the growling thunder drowned out their voices while they were astride horses. They lay in their bedrolls, both shivering now, as lightning bolts lit up the sky and thunder rumbled and echoed through the canyon walls.

He said, "We could double up. It would be warmer."

Was he suggesting they share a bedroll? "Just what do you have in mind?"

"Not what you're thinking. This is what folks do when it's cold. We put our bedrolls together. Between body heat and the extra blankets, we can make it cozy. We sleep back-to-back. I have never forced myself on a woman. If you aren't comfortable with the notion, forget I even suggested it."

She was freezing, and he made a certain sense. But could she trust herself? She had been having thoughts for the past several days about Win that she had never thought about her late husband. She worried that a slut was lurking in her body. She sighed. "This would be scandalous to most, but I guess we can try it."

Fifteen minutes later, they were burrowed into a big cocoon of blankets, back-to-back as he had promised. She was not unaware of the half-naked body next to hers, but she was warm now, and was sleepy enough to push it to the back of her mind.

"We haven't even talked about the mission. Did you get the messages?" Renata asked.

"On Mary's advice, I didn't go to The Yellow Rose, but she gave me nearly a book of information. Colonel Baker left a message with your mother. I have everything packed away, so it didn't get wet."

"I will read it tomorrow. Tell me, how was Madre holding up?"

"She seemed to be persevering well enough. Come to think of it, she seemed pretty much unfazed, except for worrying about her daughter. She is a tough lady. She was disappointed I couldn't stay the night."

"I'll bet she was." She wanted to pull back her sarcastic words the moment she uttered them, but thankfully Win did not comment. Why did she keep seeing her mother as a rival for Win's attention? She had no interest in a romance with their hired hand. "Can you give me a summary of what you learned?"

"The Rebel forces are nearly depleted at both Fort Fillmore and Fort Bliss. It sounds to me like it won't take much for the Union to reclaim them. I assume the written reports confirm what I am telling you."

"We have got to get these reports to Mexican Springs—soon. I don't know when Bodaway will return, but I don't think we can wait."

"We can wait till morning. Only a fool would ride out in this storm. If necessary, I will take the information. I guess all I've got to do is follow the Butterfield Trail."

"I could ride with you. It's treacherous country, not quite so bad, I suppose, if all the stations are still operating."

"It doesn't make sense for two of us to make that ride, and somebody needs to be here to meet Bodaway when he gets back. He doesn't know me well enough to trust me, and the two of you might be able to scare up more information."

"We can talk about it tomorrow." She suddenly felt drained, and the warmth of the bedroll was seducing her to sleep. She closed her eyes and surrendered.

When Renata woke hours later, she found herself spooned against Win's backside, one arm wrapped about his waist. Mortified, she rolled away. She listened to his breathing, steady and soft. Did he know what had happened or was he just being a gentleman? She turned over, positioning her back to him again. Renata doubted she would be able to fall asleep, but within minutes sleep claimed her and dreams offered images of her and Win that she did not find unpleasant.

It should have been sunrise when she next awakened, but a cover of black storm clouds won out over sunshine this day, and a steady rain continued, not so fierce as the night before, but unrelenting nonetheless. And she was cold, and Win was gone. Reluctantly, she wormed out of the bedroll and pulled on the only dry shirt and britches she had in her bag, thanks to her Madre who had sent the extras with Win.

But where was Win? The question was promptly answered by his appearance from the rain, water dripping off his Plainsman hat, but his shoulders covered by a crude poncho.

He slipped into the shelter, taking care not to dampen the blankets. "I had to relieve myself," he said. "Took the long side of the tarp and sliced off enough to make us two ponchos. The flap wasn't helping us rolled up on the ground. I cut a hole to slip your head through. It helps anyhow."

"I can't remember the last time I saw rain go on this long out here. Usually, we're begging for rain out in this country."

"I've been studying. It's coming from the north, too. That can't be a good sign for the river flooding."

"It's already carrying more than I have ever seen from spring mountain thaw." His mention of relieving himself triggered her own urge to pee. "Where's my poncho? I need to slip away."

Win reached behind him and pulled out a folded strip of canvas wedged between the two saddles and handed it to her. "It's not much, but it helps. You go right ahead, and I'll fix breakfast. I'm afraid I can't offer hot coffee, though."

She worked the canvas poncho over her head, pulled her hat down as low as she could, and headed out into the rain. The tails of the poncho dropped to her knees and helped considerably. She did not roam far, however, and quickly found a likely spot, completed the task, and returned to the shelter.

True to his word, Win had folded up the bedroll and laid out a pan full of breakfast on the ground. Cold biscuits and four boiled eggs. A jar of her mother's apple jam along with Win's penknife sat beside it. She sat down opposite him. "I'm glad you made the visit to Madre's. We would have starved this morning."

They each took two of the eggs, but she settled for two biscuits while Win downed three. They still had four remaining for another meal.

"I figure your mother sent us enough food for five cold meals. She was wise enough to know we might not always have the chance to cook." He lifted his saddlebags from the stack next to the saddles and plucked out two envelopes, one small and the other large and bulky. "Here is your reading for the day."

She opened the smaller one first and removed two sheets of parchment. The report was brief and precise as one might expect from an old military officer. She handed it to Win. "Read it if you like. Just as you already told me, the Confederates are undermanned at Bliss. The colonel provides numbers and locations." Mary's report was longer, naming sources and the dates her ladies procured the information. She listed a series of military complaints about depleted forces but no estimates of Rebel numbers occupying the fort and town. As she finished a page, she passed it on to Win.

Win said, "These do a good job of verifying what we already had guessed."

"When do you think we can leave for Mexican Springs?"

"You're going, too, aren't you?"

"With or without you."

"You won't be here to meet Bodaway."

"He will head for the Rough and Ready Station. He would expect Butch to know where I went. He will probably wait there till I return. You didn't answer my question—when?"

Win said, "I've been thinking. We need to see what the river is doing. The Rio Grande affects Fort Bliss, too. The water was still rising last night. The Army should know about any flooding. It looks like any attack is going to come from the west. Mesilla is on the west bank, but Fort Fillmore is on the east, and troops will need to cross the river to take the fort. The fort doesn't look like much to me, only some run-down adobe buildings lined up along three sides of a parade ground and not much in the way of fortifications in case of attack."

"The fort was mostly an outpost that sent out patrols to discourage Apache raids and was a supply link for other forts in the area. I don't think there has ever been fighting at the site. The Union troops vacated before the Confederates reached the fort. I guess they learned that the Rebels were coming with overwhelming numbers. Of course, those numbers have dwindled now."

Win said, "I think we should leave this morning. It will be a nasty slog in the rain, but I suggest we check the river and then head up the Butterfield Trail and stay the night with Butch at the Rough and Ready. You can leave word with Butch for Bodaway. I got the spyglass from Martina, so we won't need to ride in too close to get a look at the river. If the rain doesn't let up, we can wait a few extra days there, but we'll be dry."

Win was a jump ahead of her again. He seemed to forget that she was responsible for the mission. A bit grudgingly, however, she admitted that it eased her burden to be with a man who could think for himself and devise a plan. "Yes, what you say makes sense."

Chapter 28

"THE RIO GRANDE is out of its banks, overflowing mostly to the west and surrounding Mesilla. The town must be on higher ground. It looks like a moat circles the town. The river is flowing on both sides." Win handed the spyglass to Renata in exchange for the reins of both horses.

They stood on a knoll west of the river. The rain had slowed to drizzle for now, but black, menacing clouds above the mountain peaks to the north promised that they had just been granted a brief respite.

Soon, Renata gave him the spyglass. "You're right. The river has Mesilla under siege. I hope Mary's business isn't threatened."

"I doubt it. I think the east bank at Mesilla is high enough to push the water west. But you never know with flooding. The water is powerful at this stage, and you just hope the flooding stays away from you. At least, Las Cruces doesn't appear to be threatened. Anyhow, we have learned all we can here. Let's find the Butterfield Trail and make our way to the Rough and Ready."

After the riders reached the Butterfield Trail more than an hour later, rain started pouring from the sky again. They found firmer ground adjacent to the trail which had turned swampy, but now a fierce wind started to move in from the west and challenge mounts and riders. Win worried about the horses, and they reined in and rested the critters whenever they came upon a cluster of trees or stone outcroppings that provided temporary shelter. It seemed to Win they were moving at a snail's pace, but shortly after sundown he could make out the black silhouette of the Rough and Ready buildings illuminated by lightning flashes against a dark sky.

"No light in the window," Win said, "but I smell smoke. He must be there."

"Butch said he wasn't leaving. He didn't. No reason for him to have a lamp lighted, I guess. We will need to be careful about how we approach the cabin and let him know we're here. He will have several loaded rifles and a shotgun leaning against the wall."

"With this rain and thunder, he's not going to hear us call till we get to the door."

"You hold back after we near the station. I'll go to the door and knock and holler. If he looks out and sees only one up close, maybe he won't be so spooked."

"I don't have a better idea. If he doesn't recognize your voice, at least he will know it's not Charlie Hopkins."

When they were no more than fifty feet from the cabin, he heard a loud whinny from the stable and then a persistent braying, the strange sound of a half-horse and half-donkey, few of which were the same and rarely matched the sound of either ancestor. No sooner had Renata dismounted than the roar of a shotgun exploded from the front window of the adobe cabin.

"You that's afoot, raise your hands up and walk this way till I tell you to stop. You in the saddle just stay put." It was Butch's voice.

Renata obeyed and commenced walking toward the station.

When she was within nearly twenty feet, Butch hollered, "Stop. Who are you and state your business."

"It's me, Butch. Ren Rutledge."

"Ren? Well, I'll be danged if it ain't. Well, you get up here and get out of the rain. I got me a good fire going in the cookstove, and I'm betting you can use it. Is that your man friend out there? Win . . . something."

"Win Evans. We'll put the horses up and be with you soon."

"I'll unbar the door and get coffee brewing."

When Renata returned to retrieve her horse, she told Win what Butch had said. "We can finally get out of this rain. I doubt if this part of the territory has seen rain like this in human history."

"That might be a stretch, but I've had enough to do me for a long spell. You go on in and tell Butch what we're up to. I'll see to the horses."

"I should see to Spirit."

"No, go on in. I don't mind. I'll have a roof over my head."

When he led the horses into the stable, he was greeted by the mule's whinny but spared the irritating braying. After taking a few minutes to adjust his eyes to the stable's darkness, he searched out a few stalls where the roof appeared to be leaking least. There were some tattered blankets hanging on the stall partitions, and after unsaddling the horses, he wiped them down with those. He saw that the corn barrel was low, so he gave the critters no more than a few handfuls each and provided a more generous helping of hay from the stack in one corner of the stable. The theft by the Confederates of the other horses had left an ample hay supply for visiting animals.

He pulled his timepiece from his pocket and saw that it was nearly eight o'clock. It had been a long day. He hefted the saddle bags and Martina's food bag over his shoulders and ventured out into the rain again, dashing for the station door. He opened the door and shed his burden and returned to the stable to retrieve their bedrolls and other gear. The bedrolls could take some drying even if they did not use them tonight.

When he finally stepped inside, he felt like he was walking into an oven, and he savored the warmth. Renata was standing in front of the cook stove with a blanket wrapped around her, and her wet clothes, including undergarments, were hanging over a rope that had been strung across the room.

Butch sat at the little table only a few steps away, holding a coffee mug in one hand. "Howdy, Win. I got another wool blanket folded on the bed if you want to get out of your duds and hang them for drying, and there's an empty mug just waiting for your coffee."

"Thanks, Butch. Guess maybe I'll do that."

He went into the room that he and Renata had shared several days ago. The oil lamp on the bedside table had been lit but flickered now and then and furnished only a hazy light. The bundling board had been removed, but he saw the end of it sticking out from beneath the bed. He could remedy that quickly before bedtime but decided to lay out the bedrolls on the floor to dry out any dampness, thinking it might be best if he slept there.

He shed his clothes, except for his undershorts. The rain had spared them, and he was not inclined to chance displaying his bare ass and male valuables if the blanket slipped.

He walked out into the front room that served as kitchen, parlor, and Butch's trading post, clutching the blanket about his body with one hand and carrying his wet clothes with the other. Struggling with one hand, he finally got his clothes slung over the rope next to Renata's. He had spread the poncho out on the bedroom floor beside hers, figuring it should dry just fine lying there. That task finished, he pulled out a chair and sat down with Butch, who had already poured his coffee.

Win reached out and pulled Martina's food bag nearer the table and began scavenging through it, plucking out a sack of soggy biscuits and another of beef jerky and placing them on the table. "The best I can do tonight. There might be some ginger cookies in there. Have you eaten, Butch?"

"Nah, I ain't et. Wasn't planning on it. I eat when the need strikes."

And that wasn't often enough, Win thought. The man was little more than a skeleton with sagging flesh draped over his bones. Still, he did not appear feeble or ailing. Win searched some more and came up with the cookies. He placed everything on the table. "Help yourself to what's there. The cookies don't seem to have suffered much." He turned to Renata who was still huddled by the stove. "Are you going to join us, Renata?"

"I'm fine. I had coffee. Maybe I'll try a cookie later."

Her voice was soft, barely above a whisper, and she seemed pensive, her dark, brown eyes sad. Valeria had been like that sometimes, and he had learned that it was best to say nothing when a woman went quiet. He was not by nature given to moods, but he did not press those who were dealing with them.

Butch said, "I'll do hotcakes for breakfast in the morning. We'll use the last of my bacon. It's getting close to being coyote food anyhow."

"Is there a trading post at Mexican Springs that stocks food supplies? Maybe we can bring some things back. I might even buy a pack mule if I can find one."

"I'd send Molly, but she would slow you down. From what Ren told me, you ain't got time to waste."

"Yeah, that's right. It would help if the rain would quit."

"It will. Sun's coming out tomorrow. You got my guarantee."

Win wasn't going to argue with the man, but he had his doubts about the prediction. "That would help."

"Still might hit high waters at creeks and rivers along the way. The mountains ain't done pissing snow melt yet, not by a long shot."

"Is there anything else we should know about the trail going west?"

"Chiricahua would be my biggest worry. They're on the hunt this time of year. Buffaloes if they can find them, ranchers' cattle when they get the chance and any whites that look like easy kill. I swear they can smell a woman ten miles off. War party or hunting party, it don't make no difference, a woman will draw them like horse flies to a critter. Ren won't like my saying this, but she ought to stay here with me."

Win glanced at Renata whose face revealed nothing. It was almost as if she had not heard Butch's suggestion. "Renata is riding out with me. This is her mission, and she needs to talk with the contact at Mexican Springs. I'm just helping out."

He returned to eating his soggy biscuit while he had the chance. Butch had devoured four of the half dozen biscuits and was starting on the cookies. The roar of thunder shook the room's furnishings and a flash of lightning appeared so near that it looked like it might leap through the window.

Renata said, "I think I will go to bed," and disappeared into the bedroom.

Butch spoke in a voice he could barely hear, "Maybe you ought to keep her company. Something's eating on Ren tonight."

Win was surprised that the old man had picked up the signs. "She's probably just tuckered out. She's had some grueling days since we left her mother's house. But I could use a night's sleep myself."

"I'll bar the door and windows and call it a day, too. I'm usually dead asleep by now unless Molly raises a fuss. She's better than a dang dog, I'm telling you."

"I noticed tonight and the last time we were here." Win finished his coffee. He had the taste for another cup but not at this hour. The strong stuff already guaranteed he would use the chamber pot tonight. He got up and told Butch goodnight.

The old man winked. "I'm betting Ren is better in the morning."

Win shook his head from side to side. The old fart thought he had mischief in mind. He did not know how it was between him and Renata. He entered the room which was dark except for the lamplight creeping through the open door.

Renata spoke. "The lamp burned out. I think it is out of oil. Close the door."

"We won't get the heat from the front room."

"It's not that cold now that we're dried off. I've spread my blanket on the bed. You can do the same with yours. We'll be a lot warmer than we were last night, and we need to talk."

"I thought I would sleep in my bedroll on the floor. The bundling board's not up."

"We don't need the bundling board. We didn't have one last night. Now, please, come to bed."

He sighed. "I just don't think this is going to work for me. Last night was more difficult than you can know." He spread the blanket out on top of hers and crawled into the bed.

When they were stretched out on their backs, she said. "I know how difficult, but I like you near me."

"Uh, I guess that's good."

"I have been thinking."

"You were quiet out there, I thought you might be."

"I don't want another husband, not yet."

"Well, I didn't know anybody had asked." She wasn't making much sense now, and he was not certain where the conversation was going.

"I trust you, Win. I like to think we are good friends and partners now. I appreciate all you have risked for the war effort, and you stood up for me tonight when Butch suggested I stay behind."

"It wouldn't have done much good to do otherwise."

"I know. But it is getting awkward."

"It is. That's why I thought it best I sleep on the floor."

She got up on one elbow and ran the fingers from her other hand across his chest. That did it. He reached up and pulled her to him, and her face hovered over his for a moment before his lips found hers.

Their first coupling did not take long, but later they were both patient and attentive, although he worried that Butch would hear Renata's moaning. Afterward, she lay in his arms sobbing. He did not understand why, but he was confident that it was not because of regret. Finally, they both dropped into a sated sleep.

When he woke in the morning, Renata was already out of bed and the door was open just enough to let some light into the windowless room. He sat up and searched out his undershorts which had been tossed on the floor near the foot of the bed. Then he discovered his shirt and britches folded on Renata's side of the bed. Now he picked up the scent of coffee and hotcakes with a hint of bacon. He got dressed and pulled on his boots and joined the others in the front room.

Renata was in front of the stove, obviously cooking breakfast. She looked at him and smiled. He could not remember seeing her smile like that. Butch was at the table and lifted his eyebrows before he winked. The heavy wood shutters on the windows had been unbarred and were open now, and near blinding sunlight streamed through the glass. As Butch had predicted, the rain had ended. A good start to the day. He hoped it was an omen of things to come, but he was not betting on it yet.

Chapter 29

B USHWA AND NITIS sat in the shadows of rock outcroppings on sunbaked shale slopes overlooking a narrow ribbon of water that rushed through a canyon several hundred feet below. Nitis had been showing Bushwa some of the landscape outside the rancheria as he led him to the private place where he often retreated to be alone. Bushwa had an ulterior motive. He was again testing the boundaries established for his wanderings.

He had no present plans to attempt escape. Now that Nascha was carrying his child, such a decision had become more difficult. He had no intention of spending the remainder of his life with the Mescalero, but the notion of leaving Nascha and the unborn child behind was unthinkable as well. The problem was unresolved in his mind, but his hope was that he could persuade Nascha to leave the Apache at some point. There was no future among these people. Their way of life was ending, likely soon after the War of the Rebellion ended and the no-goods in Washington decided they needed somebody else to fight. Nothing changed if the South prevailed. He figured it was just a question of whether blue suits or gray suits were coming.

He looked out over the canyon and craggy stone walls that bounded it. Several eagles weaved and soared over-head, and he suspected there was a nest of eaglets in a nook in the cliffs that rose above them.

Nitis had been talkative during the journey to this place, but he had turned quiet upon their arrival. The kid was thinking about something. He would spit it out when he was ready.

Bushwa was interested in the creek below. He won-dered where it went. He had been told from childhood that if lost, follow the water. Sooner or later, it will lead you to a river and that will take you to a town. He figured that didn't count so much out west when towns could be hundreds of miles apart.

"What's that creek down there called?" Bushwa said.

"The People call it Bimisi. That means 'slippery' in the English tongue. The stones in the water are slick like ice, those who cross often fall."

"Do you know where it goes?"

"It flows to another river and then to what the Mexicans and Americans call the Rio Grande River."

It was midmorning and the sun was nearly blinding if a man moved out of the shade, so they were facing east. They could not be that far from the Texas or New Mexico Territory border to the northeast, he guessed.

"We never crossed the Rio Grande to come here."

"The band does not always travel the same way. Sometimes, we cross the river and go to the Guadalupe Mountains to stay. We often stay winters there. There is much firewood and caves for shelter there and many deer within one day's distance."

He could find his way to El Paso and then to Las Cruces if he escaped to the Rio Grande. Something to think about.

"Are you thinking of leaving the People?"

"Me? No, of course not. My wife is here."

"If you leave, I would like to go with you."

"You would run away from your people?"

"Not forever. I want to go to the white man's school and learn. I speak and write the language, but there is so much I do not know. My father says there is a boarding school in the town Las Cruces and that Indians are welcomed there. Students do work to pay for this. I hope

I can become a lawyer and return to the People to help during bad times when they are forced to reservations."

"I don't know nothing about this school or schooling, since I never been inside such a place, but it seems to me there is a lot to figure out. The place sounds like a dang prison to me. Is your pa wanting you to go there?"

"He knows what I want. I do not think he believes I can do this. My mother does not like this idea, but I do not belong here. Other boys do not like me. They think I am a white boy in Apache skin because I want to learn the ways of the white people."

"I don't know what to tell you, young feller. You got some strange hopes, I'll say that. I ain't one to stand in the way of a young pup's ambition. I'll help you any way I can. I can't promise, though, about taking you with me if I make a run for it sometime."

Nitis tensed. "We are being watched."

"What are you talking about?"

"To the north on the other side of the creek. There is someone watching us. A man standing in the trees, his black horse further back. He has something in his hands that he is holding to his face, maybe his eye. I have read of this, a telescope I think it is called."

"I see what you're talking about, but I can't make out no spyglass, and I'll take your word about the horse. You got some eyes, kid. Is he Mex or white or Injun?"

"I don't think he is Indian, but I could not say whether he is Mexican or Anglo." Nitis sprang to his feet. "Taza must be told about this." He scurried up the slope, leaving his companion behind.

By the time Bushwa reached the rancheria, Nitis was already speaking to Taza, and he joined them. Taza looked at Bushwa when he approached and said, "You see man?"

"Yep, but I can't tell you more than Nitis. He's got an eagle's eyes."

"We get horses. Show me."

Bushwa said, "A two second trip if we jump off the mountain. Helluva long ways by horseback. Don't get me wrong. I favor horses. I'd take it kindly if you'd let me ride my dapple gray." He had not been astride a horse since arriving at the Mescalero rancheria.

Taza nodded. "You ride gray horse. Nitis choose horse from Taza horse."

"I still got my saddle and tack in the wickiup. I'll snatch that up and meet you at the herds." Bushwa was enthused about having Captain's reins in his hands again. If he thought he could escape, he would race the critter away from this place, but he would not know where he was go-ing, and they would track him down for sure. But just to ride again would be a start. Building what trust he could was his best long-term hope and then waiting for the right opportunity to show up.

When he went to the wickiup to retrieve his saddle, he found Nascha on her knees beside the fire, boiling plants in a battered kettle. She was intensely studying her brew and barely noticed him pass by and enter the wickiup. She stopped him, though, when he emerged with his saddle and tack.

She got to her feet and stood. 'Where go?"

"I'm taking a ride with your brother Taza. He wants me and Nitis to help him find something." He saw suspi-cion in her eyes.

"You leave me, I find and kill you. Cut off man-parts first."

The set of her mouth indicated her words were no jest. "I'm just helping your brother, woman. I'll be back soon." He changed the subject. "What are you cooking?"

"Make tis-win. All womans make today. Drink when dark come. No afraid of bad spirits when drink tis-win."

"What is that green stuff in the pot?"

"Green stuff?"

"Some kind of plant?"

"Coyote Chaser say whites call corn sprouts, mesquite pods, and mescal. Many cactus roots. When ready pour in jugs. One moon go and People drink."

"Like tomorrow then?"

"Yes, when dark come. People like ban-jo then."

"Well, now that sounds good. Wondered if my banjo had to wait till an owl showed up again."

"Do ban-jo. Keep spirits away. Make People happy."

"Do I get to drink this tis-win? Is it like whiskey or something?"

"Not know whiskey. Nascha not drink tis-win. Make many crazy. You drink but not much."

"You are going to tell me how much I can drink?"

"Yes."

The woman wasn't giving him as much sweet talk lately, letting him know she was in charge. And danged if she wasn't. He had never let a woman lead him around by the nose like this before. He adored her most of the time, but sometimes she downright scared him. Most important, he knew that if Nascha gave him the boot, he would likely find himself tied to a torture post for a spell before the Apaches put him out of his misery. Moreover, Nascha was the one who told him what an owl di-yin needed to do to cure owl sickness.

"I'll be back soon," he said and headed for the horse herd to meet Taza and Nitis.

An hour later, after a descent along a narrow winding trail that took the riders to the canyon floor, Bushwa held the reins of the horses while the two Mescalero searched for sign in the area where the observer had been seen, at least where Nitis claimed to have seen the man. Bushwa could only shake his head and agree with the boy, because from this perspective one place looked like another to him. Besides, he was more preoccupied with climbing that narrow trail again.

Taza pointed into the trees that did not grow as thick as they did near Jefferson and back east in his home country. They spoke in Apache, leaving Bushwa without a clue regarding the conversation. Taza walked over and took his mount's reins from Bushwa and led the horse in the direction he had pointed.

Nitis joined Bushwa. "Taza believes the man to be a Mexican soldier or scout. That would be bad. He will track him to the soldiers. They could be days away—or hours. We do not know, but he will learn before he returns. We are to warn the People, but he doubts that the soldiers are nearby. The council will meet when he returns."

"And what will the council decide?"

"If we stand and fight or move to another place."

"I favor moving if anybody wants my opinion. I ain't got no quarrel with the Mexicans."

"If they attack, you will. They will either take your woman or use her before they kill her. And they will kill you, too. They hate the Apache mostly because of raids by the Chiricahua over many generations. The Mescalero harvest cattle from the ranches when it is necessary, but our band does not attack homes and women and children unless revenge is called for."

Bushwa was not certain when revenge was called for and decided not to ask. He just wanted to get back to the rancheria without riding that steep, narrow trail along the sheer mountain walls. "Is there another trail back to the village?"

"Only by going north and joining the trail you rode when you came to the rancheria. It would be almost nightfall when we returned to the rancheria."

"I would like to see this trail. Lead me that way."

The boy cocked his head to one side and studied Bushwa skeptically for some moments before he grinned. "I will show you the trail. Follow."

They mounted their horses and headed north.

Chapter 30

NASCHA HAD GIVEN him a good chewing the previous night when he and Nitis rode into the rancheria shortly after sunset. By bedtime, she had forgiven him, though, and insisted on a tumble which he would have gladly passed on until she performed her magic.

It was past high noon, and Taza had not returned yet. The villagers seemed unperturbed and caught up in their enthusiasm for the tis-win celebration in the evening. Nascha said that many saw tis-win as a messenger from good spirits that would make the People happy and protect them from all the dangers surrounding the People for several days.

Midafternoon, Bushwa went to the remuda to check on Captain. He did not sense that he was being watched as closely now and could venture out a short distance without being followed. Of course, he would not consider escape without Captain, and he was not about to ride the critter bareback. With the saddle and tack stowed in the wickiup, Nascha was still a watchdog over his imprisonment. And he did not really want to leave her and the unborn child—"Little Owl," she had declared the child would be named, boy or girl, although she had no doubt that she was carrying their son.

He paused at the edge of the mountain meadows, waved at one of the two men circling the vast herd. In his world such men would be called wranglers, guardians of the remuda. It was a huge responsibility for the riders in a culture where horses measured wealth and were relied upon for the band's survival.

His eyes scanned the mass of horses, and finally he spotted Captain, the finest horse he had ever owned. Only death could force him to part with this animal—his or the gelding's. He wondered what it would take to convince Nascha to leave her Mescalero band to join him in the civilized world. At least "civilized' was what most folks called it as the country was engaged in a war where brother was trying to kill brother. Regardless, he decided he should plant the seeds of that possibility soon. It would take time to bring her around to the idea, but he considered himself a master salesman.

He sensed movement behind him, turned his head, and saw Nitis. "You ain't going to take my scalp if you don't move quieter than that, kid."

"I was not going to take your scalp, and you should be glad of that."

"Yep. I'm hoping to get out of this yet without losing my hair."

"You wish to return to your people?"

"Yep. But I don't see how, and I don't want to leave Nascha." He hoped he was not talking too much to the boy, but Nitis was much older than his years, and for some reason he trusted the kid.

"I still want to go with you."

"Why sure, once it gets figured out, I don't know why not." But there were a thousand reasons that might not happen.

"Many are saying you will play the banjo tonight for the tis-win ceremonies."

"Yep, that's what Nascha told me. I didn't hear about no ceremonies. I thought it was just a big party."

"There will be speeches by some of the elders. The chiefs are honored with the first taste of tis-win. There will be a few prayer chants asking the good spirits to protect the People. And then the drinking will begin. The chiefs and warriors drink most, but some women will join."

"Well, it stills sounds like a big party to me. I been to more than a few of them. Got so dang drunk I don't even know how I got home. Never did find my horse one time."

"That was fun?"

"Seemed so at the time, but I got married drunk one time and that didn't work out so good, especially since it turned out she had another husband who didn't take kindly to it and beat the shit out of me. I tied the knot two more times and don't count that first one. Too bad about Sally. She was a sweetheart. It might've lasted a spell."

Bushwa noticed that the boy was not all that interested in his party adventures. "You didn't come all the ways out here just to ask about my playing the banjo. You got something else on your mind. Spit it out."

"I have a flute. I made it from the legbone of a deer."

"And you can make music with the dang thing?"

"I am not as good as the flute maker in the Two-stars clan of another rancheria, but I make music that some like. Other boys think it is foolish."

"Well, you and me are going to be a band tonight. You just sit by me at the fire circle, and we'll see what we can brew up."

Later, just as dusk was coming on, Nitis appeared at the wickiup with the bone flute. He displayed it proudly to Bushwa, who took the instrument and studied it. He could play the harmonica, with his nose even, but he knew next to nothing about flutes. He guessed the instrument to be about a foot long, and it had been shaved down as smooth as glass. The stem had three holes, and there were two notches near the top for venting he supposed. The musician obviously blew on the top of the instrument.

Bushwa's guess was that Nitis had some special artistic talent that was put into this creation. He could see why the boy was scorned by others his age. He did not seem like very promising warrior material. No, Nitis was just different. Bushwa could relate to that. He had always been the spoiled apple in a sack of fresh-picked ones and never quite found his place. Still, he doubted if anyone had more fun traipsing through life.

Bushwa never knew what song he would play and sing until it happened, and he knew Nitis would not be familiar with the music. He told the boy that he would play and sing the song and then point to him signaling that he should play a verse on the flute as best as he could. "If you want to join in anytime, I ain't got no problem with that. Just do what comes natural to you."

Nascha was busy with other women setting out tis-win jugs on blankets beyond the fire circle when Bush-wa and Nitis strolled over to the fire ring. He figured he would see his wife again when she chose.

Nitis said, "Itza-chu—Great Hawk—will be speaking first since Taza is not here. Other chiefs may say something, but I do not think they will say much. All will be anxious to drink tis-win."

Drums were beating softly now with a slow cadence, and Bushwa said, "I didn't think of this till now. We should've got us a drummer for the band. Next time, we got to do that."

The drums ceased abruptly, and a squat, middle-aged man stepped into the circle where most of the warriors had now gathered. He spoke plenty long as far as Bushwa was concerned, but it did not help that he could not understand a word the chief was saying in a voice that betrayed no emotion.

When the speech ended, as predicted by Nitis, two others spoke, and Bushwa feared he would fall asleep standing. Then the drum beating erupted into an explosion for several minutes and stopped, and a sing-song chanting began. Finally, that stopped, and Nitis said, "Now they wait for us."

The two walked into the circle and the firelight, Bushwa began strumming and singing *Pop Goes the Weasel.* He paused, pointed to Nitis who rendered a verse on the flute. Bushwa was impressed that the tune was recognizable. He was not pleased, however, with his audience which was thinning rapidly, obviously headed for the tis-win jugs. He guessed they could still hear the music from anyplace in the rancheria. He continued with *Jim Crack Corn, Old Dan Tucker, Buffalo Gals,* and a half dozen others before he took a break.

Nitis was grinning at him when they stopped for a bit. "That was fun."

"You was dang good, Nitis. You was even singing the chorus of some of them songs after listening a time or two. Your voice ain't half bad. Maybe we should take this show on the road."

"What do you mean?"

"Ain't important." He looked about, seeking Nascha's whereabouts when a pretty girl he guessed to be about sixteen years old came up to him and spoke. He looked at Nitis.

"She wants to know if you want a drink of tis-win."

"Well, I don't know why not." He smiled at the visitor, displaying the gap left by his missing front tooth.

She smiled back and handed him the pottery jug she carried. He pressed the jug to his lips and took a swallow. It was like taking fire down his throat, and he swore that his eyes crossed and that smoke shot from his ears.

The young woman said something, and he looked at Nitis.

"She wants to know if you like it."

"Tastes like what I would figure horse piss to taste like if I ever tried it. But don't tell her that. Say that I like it and thank her." Now that the tis-win had settled, he remembered that when he was a boy his first shot of whiskey had not been much better.

He looked around to be certain that Nascha was not watching and then took another good swig from the jug. He handed the jug back to the girl and nodded his head in appreciation.

"Her name is Bina," Nitis said. "It means musical instrument. She likes music, I think."

"Well, then we'll give this little sweetheart more music." He was more animated now and stepped out and danced a little jig before he started strumming the banjo and singing *Turkey in the Straw*. He performed several other tunes when he saw Bina watching him with pure adoration in her eyes. He had noticed couples disappearing from time to time, usually not with their own mates, something generally disapproved by the Apache. Maybe party time was an exception. Of course, most of the men and some of the women were staggering and falling now. Bina held up the jug and waved at him, and he skipped toward her still strumming and singing. He stopped in front of her and took the jug and swallowed. He paused, belched loudly, and took another.

Suddenly, he was struck by a dizziness and vertigo and feared he would topple over. He passed the jug back to Bina and leaned forward, placing a hand on her shoulder. Then something struck the side of his head like the kick of a wild stallion. Blackness consumed him, and he was oblivious to anything that happened after that until he woke up groggy and confused inside the wickiup, his head hurting like it never had before.

"Nascha?" Bushwa said.

"Nascha is not here." His vision was hazy, and he could not see the speaker, but he recognized Nitis's voice. "She went to her mother's wickiup and will not be back tonight. She said I should tell her if you died."

"I don't understand. Damn, that tis-win is powerful stuff. Never had any moonshine hit me like that before."

"I have never heard of moonshine, but that is not what hit you. Nascha struck you with your warclub."

"What in blazes? Why'd she do that?"

"She did not like the attention you were giving Bina."

"Bina was just offering me drinks."

"Nascha thought she was offering you more, and that you were about to take it. I do not know much about these things."

Bushwa traced his fingers over the lump on the side of his head. "Danged if she didn't wallop me."

"I said I would stay with you through the night. She will return in the morning to talk to you."

"Oh, Lord. I just want to sleep. How can I sleep thinking about that?"

"There is something else you should know."

He was fading now, maybe dying he thought, and did not care. He just wanted to disappear. "I think I'd just as soon not know more. I'm going to try dying."

Nitis ignored his words. "Taza returned. The Mexican army will probably attack within a week. The band must abandon the rancheria."

Bushwa heard him but did not reply. His eyes closed, and the pain abated as he drifted into a deep sleep.

Chapter 31

NITIS WAS GONE when Bushwa opened his eyes, replaced by Nascha who was on her knees beside him with a smile on her face. His head still pounded, but he could tolerate the pain now. He thought he would survive unless Nascha cut his throat. Maybe that is what she was smiling about.

"Good morning," he said, as he pushed away the blankets and propped himself up on one elbow, brushing the tips of his fingers over the lump on the side of his head. He thought it might have shrunk some, but it still hurt like blazes.

"You sit. Nascha give you drink."

Not more tis-win, he hoped.

Nascha disappeared and returned with a tin cup of steaming, greenish liquid. She handed him the cup and he raised it to his lips, sniffing it first. He thought he smelled mint. Regardless, it was not a repulsive odor. He sipped it first, flinching as it burned his tongue, and he instinctively blew on the brew, but soon confirmed that the taste matched the fragrant smell.

"Drink all," Nascha said.

It took him a spell, but he finally drained the cup, and his head was starting to clear. He was nervous, though, because Nascha still had not accosted him about the previous night's behavior, and he did not recall exactly what despicable acts he had committed. From the light that sifted through wickiup openings, he knew morning had arrived, but without looking at the sun against the sky, he had no notion of the time. He never liked timepieces, unlike his young partner, Win, who could not live without one in his pocket.

Nascha said, "Council meet. Fox band maybe go away."

"Leave here?" He remembered something that Nitis said about Taza returning and the Mexican army, but that was all.

"Does this have to do with the Mexicans?"

"Soldiers come. Many."

Bushwa got up. "I got to piss. Bad."

He did urgently need to relieve himself, but he also wanted to be alone to think a bit. He went into some brush just off the edge of the rancheria and unloaded what he calculated to be a gallon of water and returned to the wickiup feeling much better. He guessed from the sun's position that it must be not much after ten o'clock. Normally, he would be starved by now, but the mere thought of food made him queasy.

Nascha was outside the wickiup now tending to deer-skins stretched out on poles. The hides were not the result of his own hunting. They had been dropped at the wickiup by some unknown hunter. Others left food and other necessities to assure the well-being of the di-yins. It was not a bad set up for a man who was satisfied with mere survival, but he was starting to get bored with it.

He saw Nitis racing his way and stopped to await his arrival. The boy was nearly out of breath when he reached him.

"Hey, young feller, what's the big hurry?"

"The council has met. We are moving."

"We are? Where to?"

"Away from Mexico. Back to the United States. The Guadalupe Mountains."

"Where the devil is that?"

"You do not know? I have a map. They are in southeast New Mexico Territory and go south into Texas."

"I'll be danged. I'd be getting closer to home. If I'm thinking right, we'd have to cross the Rio Grande to get there."

"Yes. I know what you are thinking. I want to go with you, but now is not the time. You would be killed if you try."

The kid was too dang smart for his age. Before he lived among the Mescalero, his opinion of Indians placed them a step or two below horses for brains. Now he found himself wondering if they weren't as smart as whites, some maybe a hell of a lot smarter. Nitis had a mind so powerful it halfway scared him.

And Nascha could think faster than the man she had claimed for a husband. But he had learned a thing or two over the years and had a lot of faith in his own wiles. He had survived a few wars and been a clever enough tradesman and dealmaker and been called crafty more than once. He was confident he would work his way out of this mess somehow. But the time must be right.

"When do we move, do you know?"

"The day after tomorrow. Early morning. We cannot risk the Mexicans moving faster than Taza estimates."

"Dang, that don't give much time."

"The People will be ready. Many will walk. We cannot waste time. The Mexicans may give chase. I must go now and help my mother prepare to move. She will not like this, and she will worry that my father will not find us. He will."

It must be nice to have a father you looked up to like Nitis did Bodaway. He had never found much to admire in his own pa. That thought made him think of the child Nascha was carrying. Could he be like Nitis's father? Did it matter?

He walked over to Nascha who was scraping the still raw flesh off the deerskins. "Did you hear what Nitis said?"

"Some. We move."

"Yeah, and we'll be moving back up to my country as near as I can tell. I've been thinking. Why don't we strike out on our own, move to my people? The Apaches will be herded to reservations someday, or they'll be kilt off. Our child ain't got no future among the Mescalero. I like you folks and all, but I can make a better life for us in the white world."

She turned to face him with tear-glazed eyes. "Know you want leave, maybe try. Nascha not go. Little Owl not go. In white world, baby be called half-breed, never white. Here, baby be Mescalero, Fox band. I be squaw among whites, never wife. You husband and di-yin with the People."

Bushwa sighed. With the war going on, there wasn't much to return to now anyhow. He had no idea where he would go to escape it. He wondered what had happened to Win. He hoped the kid had not faced a firing squad someplace. He was a good one, and, although Bushwa was not one to look back, it would trouble him to think he had led Win off to his death.

Chapter 32

T HE JOURNEY TO Mexican Springs had been grueling, but they rode into the Butterfield Stagecoach Station midafternoon of the third day since departing the Rough and Ready. Rain and flooding of small creeks had slowed them down some, but skies had cleared now, and a near-blinding sun was baking them dry.

Renata was impressed by the accommodations here in comparison to the place where Butch Zimmer presided. There appeared to be a separate dining area for travelers and two or three lodging rooms with exterior doors offering more privacy. Perhaps they could claim a room and bed for the night and give the horses the luxury of a stable and hay, maybe even a bit of grain.

The station was located on the edge of what might be considered a small village. A trading post was nearby as well as a saloon not much larger than a chicken coop. She could make out at least four small adobe houses. Perhaps they could stay several days and resupply, buy some things that Butch might need.

She assumed that she and Win would be sharing a room and bed again. She had no idea what the future might have in store for them as a couple, but she had decided to live for today, and Win showed no inclination to pull away. Of course, why would he unless he found her repulsive? A young bachelor amidst a populace of twenty men for every woman would likely not forego an opportunity to bed any convenient female.

They dismounted at a hitching post in front of a door and boardwalk that she assumed led into the headquarters. Win retrieved the messages for the Union Army from his saddlebags and handed them to Renata. "I guess you will be doing the talking here, Ren. I'll keep my mouth shut unless somebody asks me a question."

"If you have something that you think ought to be said, say it. We're partners now. You aren't working for me anymore."

"You mean I'm fired?"

"I wouldn't put it like that. But I can't be your boss again. That wouldn't work."

"Wouldn't matter to me if I can keep my benefits."

"You've had one thing on your mind the past few days."

"Your fault."

"We'll talk if we both live through all this."

Win opened the door, and they went inside. Renata's eyes surveyed the room, which reminded her of the Rough and Ready except for a larger kitchen to the left that she assumed also connected to the dining room on the other side of the structure. To their right was a circular oak table around which three men sat, none of whom seemed to notice her, so transfixed were they by the playing cards in their hands. One, an Indian, wearing a plainsman, wide-brimmed hat, had gathered a healthy stack of gold coins near his elbow. The other two had little to show for the afternoon poker session.

One graying man with a brushy mustache wearing a Union blue shirt with sergeant's stripes on one sleeve and a kepi visored hat worked his jaws on a tobacco chaw and spat a wad in a big can on the floor before he looked up at the visitors, nodded, and tipped his cap.

"Sid," the soldier said, "you got customers."

A wiry dark-haired man with a sun-bronzed face and chin whiskers laid his cards on the table and said, "I guess we'll call it a day."

"Because you've lost your last dollar, Sid," the Indian said. "You had best be thinking of a story for Maggie."

"Let me deal with Maggie."

He scooted back his chair and stood facing his visitors. He was about Win's height but framed like a scarecrow. She guessed him to be in his late twenties, younger than many station managers. He had a nice smile, and she could see his eyes appraising her. She did not mind, glad that he was not immediately repulsed after her days on the trail.

"Howdy, folks. Welcome to Mexican Springs. What can I do for you?"

Renata said, "I am looking for Sid Varney."

"You found him, ma'am. I'm Sid."

"My name is Renata. We may need to speak privately." She spoke the code. "I come from Kansas."

His face turned serious, and his eyes narrowed in confusion. "Whereabouts in Kansas?"

"Manhattan, to the east of Fort Riley."

"I wasn't expecting you, ma'am."

"But you were looking for Bodaway?"

"Yep, we can talk, ma'am. At the table I got Sergeant Frank Hammer and Atsa Youngblood. They're both with our people. They been waiting for word from you."

Both men stood, and the soldier removed his hat and bowed. The Indian nodded a greeting.

Renata said, "This is my husband, Win Evans, and we can thank him for retrieving much of the information I have brought. We had treachery in the spy link, and the Rough and Ready has been closed down by the Confederates, as I assume Bodaway has already informed you."

Sid said, "Yes, ma'am. Butterfield is holding its coaches until the Rebels have vacated Mesilla and Fort Fillmore."

"Butch is still occupying the Rough and Ready Station. The smaller relays between here and there have been vacated and abandoned. One was burned out. We didn't try to determine whether it was Apache work or not."

"Let's all sit down and talk about this. I'll go see if Maggie has coffee brewed. I'd bet she'll find some cookies someplace, too, to help hold you to supper."

They sat down, and the sergeant spoke. "Atsa generally takes the messages from here to Fort Lowell at Tucson, but I was ordered to ride back with him this time. We're at what the colonel calls a 'critical time' and he thought an extra man would be good in case of attack along the way. Foolishness, of course, because I wouldn't do a dang thing but slow him down. He's Navajo and knows this country like the back of his hand and been relaying for a good year now. But I'm a soldier. I follow orders."

Atsa said, "I hope my sergeant friend is a better soldier than poker player. I neglected to tell him that the soldier who took me in as a three-year-old at Fort Defiance after Apache killed my parents, opened a gambling hall and tavern outside the post when he left the Army. He later married a Navajo woman who became a mother to me, and that is why we remained among the Navajo people."

Renata said, "And you attended school at the fort?"

"Yes, ma'am."

The young man had obviously known she would be curious about a Navajo who spoke English with ease and had been kind enough to satisfy her curiosity. "You have met Bodaway then?"

"Yes, we are friends. I hope he is alright."

"Yes. He made a visit to his family, and we felt that this information could not wait for his return."

Sid returned carrying empty tin mugs for coffee, followed by a young red-haired woman carrying a pot of steaming coffee in one hand and a plate of cookies in the other. She was an attractive woman but appeared somewhat haggard, probably not helped by the fact that she was obviously five or six months pregnant.

"This is my wife, Maggie," Sid said. "She was already baking some bread and says she will put on a pot of Boston baked beans with ham slices for supper—brown betty pudding for dessert."

Renata stood and placed a hand on Maggie's arm. "I will see if I can help with anything when we finish here. We can talk."

"I would like that."

"My husband and I will want to rent a room for the night. Do you have something?"

"Nothing fancy, but they're clean. These gentlemen have two of the three, but there is one waiting for you. Sid will show you."

"Wonderful. I will see you soon. I can pick up the cups here."

"Sid will do it." She shot an angry look at her husband. Maggie must be aware of her husband's gambling losses, Renata figured. She sat back down.

Sergeant Hammer commenced the discussion. "Atsa and I will saddle up at sunrise and head for Fort Lowell. California troops are arriving daily there, and the commanding officers expect to have a force large enough to move toward Fort Fillmore and Fort Bliss within a week after I return with your messages. Do you have anything to add to the reports?"

"Something that could be important is the state of the rivers. Many of the creeks and rivers east of here are flooding. More importantly, the Rio Grande River is out of its banks. Mountain snow thaws are the big culprit, but we have had more rain than I have ever seen there. The creeks and rivers can be crossed, but your scouts will need to seek out crossings where the rivers are wide and the land is flat. The currents in the narrows are fast and deadly. Certainly, this will slow troop movement, especially infantry."

The sergeant said, "The troops will be all California cavalry, ma'am. Tell me about the Rio Grande."

She turned to Win. "My husband has seen it close up and crossed it during the early flooding. Win, why don't you fill them in?"

Win was silent for a moment. She knew she had taken him by surprise.

When he responded, Win spoke very deliberately. "Several things. First, there is not much left of Fort Fillmore. The Union forces burned some of it down when they vacated. The adobe buildings were mostly gutted from what I could tell in passing and with my spyglass. I doubt that you will find Confederate troops congregated much in one place. They will likely be spread out through Mesilla. If they see a large enough force coming, my guess is they will disappear—but I'm no military strategist."

The sergeant said, "But you sound like you have been around the military."

"My wife's father is a Union colonel fighting in the east. Maybe some of his ideas rubbed off on me. Anyway, there is something I think your higher-ups should be aware of. Mesilla is on this side of the Rio Grande, of course, but I was studying the town with the spyglass before we started west to meet up with a courier here. Mesilla was surrounded by water, almost an island. It looked like the river was cutting a moat around it. I've had some experience working along rivers, and I think it's possible the Rio Grande is digging a new channel west of Mesilla."

"This seems a bit farfetched. You're saying Mesilla is going to be on the other side of the river?"

"I can't say that for sure, but since Mesilla is the Confederate capital of the territory, I assume your troops are going to want to take control of the town and raise the stars and stripes there. If so, your officers might want to be figuring out how to cross the Rio Grande if the water hasn't gone down."

"Can you keep an eye on that situation and get word to us somehow as we advance?"

Renata said, "Have someone check in at the Rough and Ready Station when the troops approach. If we're not there, we will leave word with Butch Zimmer, the station manager, about the river's status. That will give your commanders a clue about what to have your scouts looking for."

The sergeant said, "I like that suggestion, Missus Evans. We will do just that. Anything else?"

She looked at Win who shook his head "no." She said, "I think everything else is covered in the reports. Now, if you will excuse us, we need to put up our horses."

"The door to room number three is unlocked. There ain't no key or outside lock. Bolt lock on the inside, though. On each side of the door, you will see gun slots for air and defense with bolt down shutters for both. Nobody can climb through, but you can stick a gun barrel out if need be."

Atsa explained. "I told Sid that we came across a settler's place on the way here. Burned out. Man and woman and a small girl dead and scalped. From the clothing strung out, I think there was a small boy, too. They probably took him. I don't think they will attack here with the other folks that live here and most prepared to take on raiders."

Sid said, "Counting men, women, and older children of shooting age, we've got a dozen guns in our little community. Also, Apaches use the trading post sometimes, so we don't worry much about the Apache threat, just keep our eyes open and guns handy."

Atsa said, "Apache do not like night raids, but I wanted you to be aware of the war party. There could be anywhere from ten to fifteen, and you should keep an eye out on your return trip. These are Chiricahua, and there are none more dangerous and unpredictable."

Later, after they had tended to the horses and hauled their gear to the Spartan room, Win sat down on the bed and said, "It's a straw mattress but it seems soft enough, and the bed's sturdy."

"And the room is clean. I'm guessing Maggie sees to the cleaning. She seems nice but overworked, I fear."

"Most are out west."

"I suppose that's true enough." She sat down beside him.

"Thanks for the promotion," Win said.

"What do you mean?"

"From stable hand to husband. I'd say I've done quite well the past several months."

She turned her flushed face toward him. "I'm sorry. I don't know why, but I was embarrassed in front of strangers to admit we were not married and wanted to share a room—I guess we did anyway?"

"Of course. I'm getting used to you sleeping next to me. It will be a hard habit to break someday."

For some reason, she felt a sense of panic at the thought of their separation, which she guessed was inevitable. "Well, you adapted very easily to the little lie and added one yourself. You have never even met my father."

"I swear I don't make a habit of lying, but I learned the art of a story from the best—Bushwa Sparks." He reached over and pulled her to him, pressing his lips gently to hers.

She felt her heart racing and the desire stirring in her loins. She pulled her head back and met his greenish-blue eyes, certain they were laughing at her. He knew. "I promised to help Maggie with supper."

"It doesn't take us long," he said.

This time, she leaned over and kissed him, lingering and brushing the tip of her tongue softly to his lips. She began unbuttoning his shirt, then paused again. "The door."

"It's bolted."

"You devil. You planned this, didn't you?"

"I confess."

"Well, let's not waste any more time."

After supper, Seargeant Hammer and Asta disappeared, apparently deciding to grab sleep for an early departure. Renata had found the Navajo an interesting young man with concerns beyond the war. This was to be his last mission before returning to his people, for whom he hoped to act as a spokesman because the Army was considering plans to remove the Navajo from their homelands. A representative fluent in both English and Navajo would be vital to the cause.

The sergeant, on the other hand, had no plans beyond the Army. He was a soldier and would be until he died or was forced into retirement someday. For now, he was focused on his current assignment—getting the intelligence she had gathered to his superiors.

Renata and Win helped Sid and Maggie with clean up, sat and chatted with them over coffee for a short time, and then, agreeing to stay for several days, excused themselves and went off to their room. They undressed, fell into bed, snuggled together and Win fell instantly to sleep. It was just nice to have him near, she thought. She felt more married to this man than she ever had to the one she married. She would not allow herself to use the word "love," but she had never felt more at ease with a man. Sleep quickly claimed her.

She woke when she heard voices outside. She got up and peered through the gun slots just in time to see the couriers ride away. They had said their goodbyes last night, but she felt lazy not having arisen to see them off. The least she could do would be to help Maggie with breakfast. She was a sweet thing just barely eighteen years old, and she loved her husband, but she had confided that he did not handle money well. Of course, Renata had witnessed that when the poker game was finished yesterday.

Maggie also had whispered to her last night that Atsa had given her the money he won from Sid with an admonition to hide it. And she would until she needed it for food supplies at the trading post. It was not good for couples to have these secrets but sometimes it was a necessity, Renata thought. Maggie was lonely here and frightened about the prospect of birthing a baby with no physician within a hundred miles. She was grateful that there were two other women at Mexican Springs who had promised to help when the time came.

Renata wished she could offer Sid and Maggie employment at the business in Las Cruces, but her own life was uncertain while this war continued, especially when the Confederates were in charge. She did invite them to come and visit when the Confederates left the territory and promised to provide at least some temporary work if they wanted to seek other opportunities. She knew her mother would take the family in, provide a place for them. Dogs and cats were not the only strays she took in.

Renata was dressed now and could awaken Win. She was sure that if he had seen her unclothed, he would have tried to lure her back to bed, not that she would not have ordinarily been willing, but she had made promises to Maggie.

She walked over to the bed and gently shook his shoulder. "Win, time to get up. I'm going to see if I can help Maggie with breakfast. After we eat, we can go to the trading post. Then, Maggie has some projects I said I would assist her with while we're here. Maybe you can find something to do with Sid."

Win rolled over onto his back and looked up at her with a scowl on his face. "I don't think he's got any poker money."

Chapter 33

THREE DAYS LATER, an hour after sunrise, they rode away from the station, Sid and Maggie standing outside the stable and waving them goodbye, the latter with tears streaming down her cheeks. During their brief time together, Renata had formed a friendship with the young woman and wished that she lived nearby.

They rode the horses at a slow trot for the first few miles, then quickened the pace along the Butterfield Trail for several hours before coming to a swollen stream and reining in to rest horses and riders. They dismounted and led the mounts to the streamside to drink. Yucca, creosote bushes, and agave were plentiful on the desert landscape that surrounded them, but there was not a single shade tree in sight to ward off the heat of a searing sun approaching high noon.

Win said, "We're lucky for the flood waters right now. I'm betting this is a dry streambed most of the year."

"Yes, you can barely make out the purple haze of mountains to the north that are feeding this one. Another week, and this will be bone dry."

"Ren, look south. Do you see that dust cloud moving this way?"

"Yes, and that's no whirlwind."

Win plucked his spyglass from the saddlebags and focused on the dust. "It's not a column like you would expect of soldiers. We'd best get moving."

As they mounted their horses. Renata said, "You think they're Apache, don't you?" Fear sent a wave of weakness through her body and gnawed at her stomach for several moments. She was not ready to die, especially not like this.

They reined their mounts across the stream in water that was nearly a yard high at its deepest. When they were on dry ground again, Win pressed the telescope to his eye. "They are Apache. I don't know how they sighted us from that distance, but I doubt they would be riding like they are if they weren't after somebody. They'll eventually run us down. We've got to find a place to make a stand."

"Remember that spiny, stone ridge out in the middle of the flatlands not far off the trail? You said it reminded you of an alligator snapping turtle like you used to see back in Iowa—a giant one. You thought you saw a path leading to higher ground and wished you had time to explore it."

"Let's ride. It can't be more than a mile or two."

They pushed the horses to their limits. When they approached the stone formation that erupted from the earth for a mile or more, Renata tossed a look over her shoulder and was horrified to see that the Apache were closing the gap significantly, now not more than a hundred yards behind them.

When they reached the base of the ridge, they dismounted, and Win hollered, "Grab canteens, rifle, and saddle bags, slap your mare's butt, and head up the path. I'll follow you."

It was insane giving up their horses in this barren land, she thought, but what choice did they have? She had no notion of where the path led, but they would be on high ground, and the walls were too steep on this side of the ridge for the pursuers to take another route. They could not withstand a long siege, but if they could find cover, it would be nearly impossible for the Apache to swarm them.

She headed up the narrow path and was nearly out of breath when she heard gunfire behind her and turned. Win, damn him, was far behind her, trying to hold off the attackers who had dismounted and were rushing toward him. She estimated a dozen of them, although one was stretched out on the ground. There appeared to be only a few rifles, but arrows were flying now. She readied her rifle and started a shower of lead. Two Apache fell, and the others backed off a bit.

Win turned and started dashing up the trail again, but he appeared unsteady on his feet. And then she saw that the front of his shirt was covered with blood.

"Win," she yelled, "you're injured. I'm coming back to help."

"No, I'll catch up. You just keep firing. Keep them off the trail. I'm out of range for their bows, and all they've got are single shot rifles."

She kept firing, and the Apache moved back some and appeared to be conferring about something. Soon, five warriors returned to their horses and rode away, staying close to the base of the ridge. This worried her because she could not imagine them surrendering that easily.

Win was staggering by the time he reached her, and she stifled a scream when she saw the arrow imbedded in the left side of his chest. "Win, my God, you can't go any farther."

"Got to. Look for cover up ahead while I rest a spell. I can fire my Spencer yet. I can hold them off for a spell if they head up the trail again." His voice was raspy now.

Renata hated to leave him, but she needed to find a place they could defend. Rocks and small boulders made the footing tricky. The trail widened and the path snaked easterly along the top of the ridge. She could see no natural fortress along the scalped ridgetop which was naked of vegetation except for scattered patches of sagebrush. A cluster of stones and a gully slicing through earth offered the only prospect. She could roll stones along the gully's edge to give them more cover.

They would not be more than twenty-five feet from where an Apache would come over the crest before the trail fanned out. They could still maintain an edge, if she could get Win up here. The crack of his rifle told her he still lived.

She dropped her saddlebags and canteen near the gully and headed back down the trail to summon Win. She was surprised to find that he had climbed almost half the remaining distance to the ridgetop since she left him, now leaning against a boulder along the path overlooking the Apache who had moved back on the narrow trail that forced them to climb single file. She could only count three now, so she assumed Win's rifle shots had not been wasted. But where were the other warriors?

She knelt beside Win. "I found a place. It's not the best, but we can make it work. How can I help you?"

"Take my rifle and saddlebags and help me to my feet. Lead the way. Keep an eye out for what the Apache are doing. If they start to close the gap on us, we'll stop and feed them some more lead slugs."

His face was ghostly pale, the flesh about his eyes dark and sunken. The arrow shaft protruding from his chest and his shirtfront soaked with red and browning blood helped make him a frightening visage. A sense that they could not survive this consumed her, yet more determined to battle on.

"Let's get moving," Win said. "Bushwa always says it ain't over till it's over."

He had evidently sensed her despair, but she had no time to ponder the profundity of those words. She stood, offered him her hand and helped him to his feet. With the saddlebags tossed over one shoulder and a rifle in each hand, she started back up the steep path.

She could hear Win's labored breathing behind her. This was just too much in his condition, and she was tempted to stop and make a stand right where they stood.

She paused and looked back. She saw the Apache hurrying up the slope behind them now. She stepped aside and said, "Win, keep going if you can. I'm going to slow those devils down."

He protested, "I won't go on without you."

"Oh, shut up and get your ass moving. I'm in charge now. Do what I tell you."

He blinked in surprise before nodding and staggering on. She set down Win's rifle and dropped the saddlebags and aimed at the first Apache on the trail, perhaps nearly 150 feet distant. She fired two shots. He fell back against the others, still maintaining his balance but obviously hit somewhere. The wounded warrior stumbled to the rear, and the one who replaced him froze. She figured they would hold up till there was more distance between them.

She snatched up the other rifle and saddlebags and was surprised to see how far Win had gone. He appeared to be moving like a crippled turtle, but he was nearing the ridgetop. By the time she caught up with him, he had reached the summit and fallen to the ground.

"Over there," she said, pointing to the gully and cluster of stones. "Can you make it?"

"Get my stuff over there. I'll crawl if I've got to." And he did, while Renata commenced rolling and stacking stones along the edge of the gully which she estimated was no more than three feet deep.

When Win made it to the gully, she helped him down the slope to the trough. "We'll make our stand here," she said.

"Guess we got to. I'd tell you to make a run for it, but I don't know where you'd go."

"I wouldn't leave you, Win. Never." And she meant every word.

"Hand me my Spencer. They'll be coming over the hump any minute."

She gave him the rifle but doubted if he could even stand. Win struggled to his feet and pushed his rifle barrel between several stones, keeping his head low. Renata, less than five feet to his right, readied to fire. The first Apache's head appeared over the ridge. He hesitated, his eyes seeking his quarry. Then they fixed on the pitiful fortress where Win and Renata were positioned. He turned his head and spoke to his tribesmen just before Win squeezed his rifle's trigger and drove a slug into his neck, and he collapsed on the path.

"That will keep them back a spell," he said.

A few minutes later, a gun roared and sent a missive that kicked shards and dust off one of the rocks on their fortress. Then an arrow arched above them and fell behind the gully. The other warriors were belly-crawling from the opposite side of the ridge which obviously offered easier access, some protected by scattered stones. Renata could not find a good target but fired in the direction of the newcomers. She was surprised that Win had not fired and glanced his way. He was no longer in firing position. His body was crumpled in the gully's trough, unmoving and silent. She was not certain he was breathing.

"Win? Do you hear me? Win?"

No response. It would be over soon. For a moment she considered snatching Win's pistol from its holster and ending her own life rather than being taken by the Apache. She had heard the horror stories of women who had been taken by the Chiricahua. Only the lucky ones lived to become a slave or squaw.

She gripped her rifle and returned to her position only to see an angry warrior running toward her with war axe raised. He was only eight or ten paces away. She would never get a shot off in time. A rifle cracked from behind her, striking the attacker dead center in the chest, and he stumbled a few steps, released his hold on the axe and dropped to the ground only a few steps from his destination. The rifle from behind her fired again, and another Apache fell.

She joined the battle again. She hit another warrior who disappeared downslope in retreat. The others joined him, as the gunfire from behind became more rapid, sounding like the attack of a small army. Finally, there was silence on the ridgetop. Renata turned to search out the rifleman who had come to their aid and saw Bodaway rise to his feet and emerge from behind a thicket of sagebrush.

She gave him a wave of acknowledgment and dropped immediately to Win's side. Her fingers trembled as she placed them on his cheek. She was still uncertain if he was alive. His head moved slightly at her touch, and a soft moan came from closed lips.

"Win? Can you hear me?"

He did not reply, but he was alive. Just minutes earlier she had resigned both herself and Win to death, and then Bodaway appeared and within minutes restored hope. She desperately wanted Winston Evans to remain a part of her life. But what could she do? She had doctored mules and horses since she was a child, but she had never dealt with human wounds before, and an arrow shaft protruding from a man's chest was more than a formidable challenge.

Bodaway's presence was announced by the shadow cast over the occupants of the gully, and she looked up at the grim-faced Mescalero standing above her. The Apache said, "He lives?"

"For now. Can you help him?"

Bodaway joined her in the crevice and bent over Win. He grasped Win's legs, and his powerful arms easily straightened the twisted form. He knelt, and his fingers probed the swollen flesh about the protruding arrow. Then he clutched the shaft with both hands and snapped it, leaving only a stub sticking from the entry place now.

The Apache said nothing, and Renata could not resist pressing. "Will he live?"

"No can say. Get arrowhead out. Not deep but Chiricahua war arrows have poisons sometimes. Bad spirits come to wounds and kill."

He pulled his skinning knife from its sheath and pressed the point next to the shaft stub. She felt faint when the blade cut its way into the wound and fresh blood began to ooze.

Minutes later, he yanked on the stub, and the arrowhead pulled free followed by a spurt of blood. "Arrowhead not so big. That good." He pointed to the kerchief about her neck. "Put to wound."

She removed the kerchief and folded it into a square, wondering about the dirt and sweat that covered it. She had never heard that such things mattered, but common sense told her that a clean compress would be better, not that she had anything on her person that would qualify. She pressed the cloth to the wound that did not seem to be bleeding so much now.

They needed to bind the compress somehow, and she remembered a coil of rawhide that Win carried in his saddlebags. She sliced off two lengths for double bindings to secure the compress just below his ribcage where the arrow point had entered. She looked at Bodaway. "But now what do we do?"

"We go to east away from Chiricahua. They come back for dead and not follow."

"But how do we move Win?"

"Hide horses. Get down from here, then see."

"You have more than one horse?"

"See your horses come from here. I catch and come find you."

"You saved our lives. I will never forget that." She hoped that included Win's. "Shall we get him out of this gully?"

"You take legs, and we bring him out."

Win was not a small man, but Bodaway wrapped powerful arms about his shoulders, and Renata took his feet and legs, and they got Win to more level ground. They set him on the rocky surface, leaning his back against a boulder, so he could sit with Renata's assistance.

Bodaway said, "Give Win water now. See if he help us."

She retrieved their canteens and saddle bags from the makeshift fortress while Bodaway steadied Win.

"Am I dead?" It was Win, his voice not much more than a croak.

She knelt beside him with the canteen in one hand, the other lodged behind his neck to assist with drinking. "Win, you need to drink. You lost a lot of blood."

"Are you my wife?"

"No, I'm your friend, Ren."

"Are you going to kiss me?"

"Of course." She gave him a chaste kiss on his cheek. "Now you must drink." She pressed the canteen to his lips, and to her surprise he drank greedily. She pulled the canteen back, deciding he should drink in small amounts to start with. Bodaway nodded approval.

"I remember you now, Ren," Win said. "You took me to heaven for a visit."

He was talking nonsense, but she did not care for the direction of the conversation. "Win, we must get you to our horses, but that means we will be walking down a steep trail. Bodaway and I can help you, but it will be much easier if we don't have to carry you. I would like to see if you can stand. We will help."

"Bodaway? Is he your husband?"

Win was obviously very confused. "No, he is not my husband. He is a dear friend who saved our lives."

"Do you have a husband?"

"No. Now let's see if we can get you to your feet."

"Will you marry me, Ren?"

The man was insane. "We will talk about this another time." She gestured to Bodaway to get on the other side of Win, and they each grasped him under a shoulder and lifted, Bodaway lifting the greater part of the load but receiving unexpected help from Win, who showed some strength in his legs. When he was standing, she offered him more water, and he took it effortlessly this time.

She worried that they would be forced to abandon some of the guns, but Bodaway handed her rifle to her and bound Win's Spencer and the saddlebags together with the remaining rawhide cord. He hoisted the bundle over his shoulder and, clutching his own rifle, moved next to Win. With Renata and Bodaway each supporting him, Win took several tentative steps.

"Can you walk?" Renata asked.

"I think so, but don't expect me to dance."

Chapter 34

THE DESCENT FROM the ridge was slow and grueling, with many pauses to rest. Renata saw that Win drank at each stop. Win noticeably weakened as the minutes passed, and by the time they reached the ridge's base Renata and Bodaway were nearly dragging him. They eased him to the ground, and then without a word Bodaway disappeared.

Win's canteen was dry now, and Renata helped him drink from her own. Bodaway had said there was a spring at the far west end of the ridge where they could water the horses and replenish their own supplies. Bodaway wanted to travel through the night to put as much distance between the Chiricahua and themselves as possible and to get Win to the Rough and Ready Station.

Night travel would be cooler, and most Apache would be reluctant to pursue at night because of bad spirits, ac-

Ron Schwab

cording to Bodaway, although he seemed unconcerned about nocturnal dangers. Her concern was whether Win could ride or not. They had no trees here with which to fashion a travois, however, during their journey to Mexican Springs, she had noticed a cluster of cottonwoods along a flooding creek bank. Bodaway had seemed confident, however, that he could secure Win to a horse with tether ropes they were using to stake out their mounts.

She sat down beside Win, who appeared to be half asleep, his head drooping forward with chin resting on his chest. "Win, do you think you can ride?"

"The arrow's gone."

"You just figured that out? Bodaway removed it. He said it wasn't terribly deep." She unbuttoned the front of his bloody shirt to check the compress. It was blood-soaked, of course, after the rugged journey down from the ridgetop. Since the bleeding was not profuse, she was reluctant to tamper with it now. Perhaps, when they went to the spring, she could wash it and make a new compress from a portion of her shirt.

She said, "You didn't answer my question. Can you ride?"

"Have to, I guess."

"Are you in a lot of pain?"

"Enough that I'm not looking for more."

She could not help him with that. Miles astride a horse's back were not going to bring less pain. "Bodaway plans to hitch you to your horse, so you won't fall off."

"What horse? We turned Buddy and Spirit loose."

"No, remember, Bodaway found them. He should be back with the horses soon."

"Oh, that's right."

His mind was still not working right, but she supposed that was to be expected. She was rescued from their clumsy conversation when Bodaway appeared, leading three saddled horses. "Chiricahua go west with dead," he said. "Not follow. Too many dead. Guns old and warriors no shoot good. We kill if come."

Win did not protest when they half lifted him onto his horse and hardly seemed to notice when Bodaway hitched him to Buddy and the saddle like a bundle of supplies to a pack mule. His arms and hands would be free to hold the reins, but it appeared unlikely that he would. A lead rope on his horse made it irrelevant. He unnerved her a bit when he said, "Don't bury me if I die. Just cut me loose and leave me behind. I like this country. I'd just as soon be a part of it."

She scolded him. "Don't talk like that. You're not going to die."

Ron Schwab

"We'll see how it turns out. Right now, I just want to sleep." He leaned his head forward, resting it against his gelding's neck and closing his eyes.

She sliced some strips from the tail of her shirt and changed the compress at the spring. The flesh about the wound was scarlet and swollen. Bodaway looked at it solemnly and said nothing to allay her fears.

Darkness descended on the desert several hours later, but a starlit night and half-moon provided sufficient light for following the Butterfield Trail. They rested the horses from time to time, but the slow pace did not tax the animals. Several times, Bodaway departed to backtrack and reconfirm that the Chiricahua were not following.

As they came to the flooding creeks and rivers that offered dry beds most summers, she thought the water flow had receded some. Several were back within their banks, although running nearly full. Regardless, Bodaway knew the country and found relatively easy crossings.

They snatched brief snoozes during the day and rode most of the second night again, hoping to reach the Rough and Ready by morning following the third night. Win was not faring well, and she tried to prepare herself for his death, knowing that it was possible. Somehow, she had bonded with this young man in a way that made him more than a partner and lover. The thought that he would exit from her life was devastating, and she fought to keep her emotions from crippling her.

The afternoon before they hoped to cover the last stretch that would take them to the Butterfield Station by sunrise of the next day, Win burned with a fever and dropped into unconsciousness. The wound was oozing pus and stank now, telling his comrades that corruption had invaded. She reminded herself, however, that this was not a sign of imminent death among mules and horses and could be a sign of internal healing. She took Win's penknife and opened the wound that had been scabbing over and drained a river of pus and rancid blood.

Win groaned which gave her a thread of hope. With scrub trees nearby, Bodaway had lashed together a travois and covered it with Win's blankets. Buddy could pull his owner in the stretcher-like rig now, and Win's body could lie flat instead of crumpled in the saddle. The arrangement would not eliminate the putrefaction of the wound, but it should greatly enhance his comfort, she hoped.

When sundown approached, they hitched the travois to Buddy and eased Win onto his crude ambulance. Renata led Buddy while Bodaway still scouted the perimeters for any threats. It seemed a long night with many stops, but she was encouraged by Win calling her name several times and drinking water when they reined in the horse.

She wanted to get him to a physician, but there were none in Mesilla and only one crotchety old man in Las Cruces who would certainly not ride as far as the Rough and Ready to see a patient even if it were possible to cross the flooding Rio Grande. Perhaps Butch Zimmer had picked up a few medical skills over a long lifetime in barely civilized lands.

The party arrived at the Rough and Ready Station well ahead of sunrise. As they approached, Molly, the mule in the stable, started braying.

Soon, one of the indoor window shutters came part-way open, and Butch hollered, "Who goes there?"

Renata called back, "It's Ren and Bodaway with Win. He's hurt bad."

The door opened, and Butch stepped out with a lantern. "Ren, you take the lantern, I will help Bodaway haul this travois into the bedroom. What happened?"

"Apache arrow. It's a long story."

"The story will hold. Let's get him inside."

By sunrise, Win was in bed. Butch had done more cleaning of the wound, digging at decaying flesh more ruthlessly than Renata had, then rinsed it with whiskey.

The bleeding increased some, and he put a few spoons of gunpowder in the wound. "I've got some horse salve I got from the vet in Mesilla we can use in a few days to help the healing."

She questioned whether Win would live long enough for the horse salve treatment, but Butch's words gave her renewed hope. "Is there anything else we can do?"

"Yep. Help me fix a decent breakfast. Y'all are looking on the gaunt side. Then we're going to see if we can get that man in there to eat and maybe even take a sip of my coffee. That'll wake the dead, I tell you. Sorry, ain't a good choice of words, I suppose."

"Do you really think he's going to live?"

"Dang right. I ain't lost a patient yet. You just do what old Butch says."

Bodaway slipped away to the stable to get some sleep. They had agreed on the ride to the station that he would scout the status of the Rio Grande and report back, so they could update the Army if troops stopped at the station as Sergeant Hammer had advised at Mexican Springs.

She was surprised when she and Butch went into the bedroom with a mug of coffee and a plate with a few syrup-soaked hotcakes and found Win awake albeit confused and groggy. She was almost giddy when she saw the new alertness in Win's eyes. She went over to his bed-side and kissed his cheek. "Feeling better?"

His voice still weak, he said, "Some maybe. I smelled coffee and hotcakes. That woke me up. Thought I was in heaven. Maybe I am."

"Can you eat?"

"I'll try."

"A drink of water first. We've got to get water in you. I don't remember the last time you peed, but it was almost orange. That's not good."

"You helped me piss?"

"You couldn't help yourself. I was honored."

"Oh, Lord, I'll bet."

"Well, get better, and you can take care of that your-self. We've got a chamber pot in here."

He took a healthy drink of water and ate half the hotcakes that she forked into his mouth. Sip by sip, he downed the entire mug of coffee with Renata holding the cup. His hands were still too shaky to control a cup and utensils. When he finished, he dropped instantly to sleep. Butch left the room, and she took his advice, pulled off her boots, slipped out of her britches and crawled into bed beside Win, knowing that sleep would arrive quickly.

"Ren?"

"What, Win. I thought you were asleep."

"Felt you crawl in with me. Just wanted to know if you've thought about it."

"Thought about what?"

"If you'd marry me. You said you would think about it."

She had not supposed he even remembered asking her. He had been delirious then. "I think I said we would talk about this another time."

"And?"

"I'll marry you if that's really what you want."

"Hoped you would." He slipped back into his slumber. Renata joined him quickly.

Chapter 35

BUSHWA WAS PUZZLED about the move of the Mescalero band from Mexico and what it meant to his future. He supposed it would not affect his status as owl di-yin and that he had a home among the band for so long as he did not attempt to escape. And that was the word—"escape"— for he did not consider himself a tribesman, and he was a prisoner. He would never be an Apache.

But Nascha would not leave her people, and as much as he tried to convince himself that he could persuade her otherwise, deep down he knew he would not. And the baby? He had never had a child before, at least not one that he'd ever met or known about. He was not a man unduly plagued by conscience, yet on occasion a sense of responsibility imposed obligations upon him. He was loyal to his few friends, and Nascha and the unborn child called to that small part of him. He would talk with her again tonight. Maybe they could do a little horse trading, each give a bit.

All but their shared blankets were bound with rawhide strips for travel. Many items would be abandoned, and these people seemed to accept it all as a matter of course. This would be their last night in the wickiup, and Bushwa admitted to a bit of sadness at leaving the place behind. It had become as much home as he had ever had. He had been something of a nomad all his life, but his new destination had always offered trading posts and shops and the promise of profit and excitement that usually did not threaten a man's life.

Nascha had turned quiet ever since he first broached the subject of her leaving the band to move to the white man's world. She shared his blankets, but no longer invited his lovemaking, sleeping with her back to him, wearing her skirt and blouse. He supposed if he approached her, she would couple, but the enthusiasm would be absent, and his itch wasn't that bad yet.

Tonight, before they crawled into their blankets, Nascha initiated the conversation. "You not stay with Mescalero."

"I didn't say no such thing, sweetheart."

"Nascha know what you want. I not kill you. Taza maybe."

"Nascha. Come with me. Try living in my world. You might find you like it. If you are unhappy there, I will bring you back to your band. If you ain't willing to do that, I'd be willing to come back and forth. Bodaway sort of does that. Has himself a foot in both worlds. I could still be part of my child's life. Things are changing. You know they are. Maybe you'll change your mind someday, or maybe I will."

"Never leave People."

"Dang it, Nascha. We got to work this out."

"Nascha sleep."

He concluded their talk was over when she turned away and crawled into their blankets. Let it rest a spell. They would talk in the morning. He did not figure he would be trying to escape anytime soon, but she was right. He did not intend to spend the rest of his life pretending to be Apache.

Bushwa woke in the middle of the night to total silence. He reached out to touch Nascha, but she was not there. Sometimes she would disappear in the middle of the night for a short time to talk to the owl spirits, so he did not give it much thought. When he got up shortly af-

Ron Schwab

ter sunrise, she was gone, but she always rose before he did.

Still only half awake, he stumbled away from the wickiup to relieve himself in the trees that fringed the rancheria. He still tended to avoid what he called the "common pissing ground."

When he returned to the wickiup, Nascha still was not there. Taza's younger wife showed up with a bowl of some sort of mush for breakfast. He asked about Nascha, and she did not understand—or claimed she did not anyhow. He dipped into the mush with his fingers and began sucking off the tasteless stuff. He longed for a place that had spoons, and his belly was crying for a real breakfast of eggs and sausage or bacon, maybe some fried potatoes, and, of course, hot, black coffee. Real food. He would bet he had lost twenty pounds since coming to the Mescalero rancheria. Luckily, he carried a mite extra. But he was going to waste away to skin and bones if he didn't get civilized food soon.

Bushwa could feel it in his bones. Something wasn't right, and it made him nervous. The women were rushing about and tying skins, blankets, and other possessions into manageable bundles, and it reminded him to pack his own things. He decided to take the buffalo hide and blankets, and, certainly, his guns and banjo. He had assumed Nascha would do his packing, and he had not been accustomed to looking after himself of late.

When he had all his worldly possessions outside the wickiup, he wondered if he could retrieve Captain from the remuda. He sure as the devil did not want to try to walk with this load. It would be worse than the infantry he had escaped from. He knew the band was pulling out from the rancheria this morning, but no one was telling him anything. That woman of his should be taking care of these things, and it made him angry and edgy.

He was relieved when he saw Nitis walking in his direction. The boy always seemed to know what was going on, and it would be a relief to speak to somebody who talked a real language.

"Good morning, Nitis," he said when the boy reached him. "I'm sure glad you come by."

"We leave soon. We should go claim your horse from the remuda."

"Will the guards let me, you think?"

"I believe so. You are the owl di-yin. They would not likely question you since we will be leaving soon. Do you have your saddle?"

"In the wickiup."

"Come. I will help you."

During the walk to retrieve Captain, Bushwa asked. "You ain't seen Nascha, I suppose?"

"You did not know?"

"I know I can't find her."

"She is gone."

"Gone? Gone where?"

"She left with Taza before sunrise."

"I don't understand."

"I think you are now what your people call 'divorced.'"

"That's all there is to it? She just leaves?"

"Yes, but usually she just returns to her family."

"That makes sense. So where did they go?"

"She will live with another band, for now anyway."

"How will I find her?"

"I am sorry. You will not, unless Taza decides to tell you. I fear he will not."

"But she is carrying my child."

Nitis shrugged.

They were not challenged when they cut Captain from the remuda. Others were claiming their horses for the journey ahead, and the chaos seemed to make Bushwa invisible. When they returned to the rancheria, Nitis helped Bushwa saddle the gelding and anchor the salvaged belongings to the dapple gray.

"Where is your horse?"

"My mother will ride with my little brother and sister. My father has the only other horse, so I will walk. Many will walk."

"I figured your pa would have lots of horses."

"No. He has worked for the white solders for many years. He has not been here to participate in raids to steal horses. He is only tolerated among the People. Some think he is a traitor. My father would leave to make his way among the whites, but my mother will not go with him."

"I guess I ain't the only one with such troubles. When Taza gets back, I will be having a talk with him about Nascha."

"Nascha gave you certain protections. Some do not think a white man can be a true di-yin. You must take care with what you say to Taza. Show him that you have your powers without her. Do you know why she divorced you?"

"She was convinced I would try to return to my own people. I tried to talk her into coming with me, and I offered to do like your pa does—go back and forth. She would not have it."

"Taza knows you will try to leave. That is not good. They will not want to risk upsetting any spirits now. I

Ron Schwab

think you will not be harmed while we flee the Mexican soldiers."

"But once the escape has been made?"

"The council members will meet, and Taza will consider their thoughts. But since he brought you here and his sister divorced you, the decision is his."

"I'm not liking them odds just now."

"I will help you escape when the time comes, but you must take me with you."

"But I can't raise you up, see to the book learning you want."

"My father said he knows someone I could stay with if I choose to leave the band. He told me I should go to a place called the Rough and Ready on the Butterfield Trail and wait for him there if I leave before he is ready to help me. He wants me to wait until I have reached sixteen years and have the right to choose, but he feared I would not wait."

"But you risk being kilt if you go with me and get caught."

"I would be punished but not likely put to death. Some would prefer to see me gone. I have no friends here and do not enjoy war and hunting games. I am accurate with my bow and have killed deer and other animals so that my family might eat, but I am sickened by the thought of killing and scalping even those who are considered en-emies. I took no pleasure in the killing of the scalp hunt-ers. White men would say I do not have the makings of a warrior."

"Take my word for it kid, being a warrior or soldier ain't all it's cut out to be. I got to admit that your good sense scares me some, though. Yeah, I'll take you with me. Hard for a man with near forty years under his belt to admit that some kid is his best chance of getting out of this place. You just tell me when the time is right."

Chapter 36

TAZA RETURNED TO the Fox band three days following his departure with Nascha. By this time his tribesmen had vacated the rancheria, and a broken and scattered column of some eighty to ninety Mescalero had descended from the mountains and now trudged northward over the desert-like landscape.

The warriors and small children, two or three astride a critter, enjoyed the comfort of a horse. Most of the women and older children—especially females—walked, shoulders bearing their sole possessions. Some of the feeblest women were placed on horseback. A husband and wife had wandered away to die. Coyote Chaser had told Bushwa that this was the Apache way and that others would choose death before the journey ended.

Coyote Chaser rode beside him now, their horses moving at a walk. Bushwa considered the man a friend but one who placed careful limitations on the friendship. The coyote di-yin would stop short of risking his own life or social status to help a friend, but recognizing that limitation, Bushwa could still mine assistance from him.

Bushwa said, "Taza has been back two days now and ain't spoke a word to me. Think he's fixing to have me tied and roasted on a stake?"

"Taza is troubled. He does not know what to do about you. Nascha does not want her child's father killed. He and others are fearful of killing a di-yin, but some say you are a fraud and that you are no longer Apache since you have been divorced by your wife. They want you tortured and killed and tied to the back of your horse and released near a settlement as a warning to other whites."

"That ain't exactly a notion to cheer me up. Being a di-yin is sort of like being a politician, ain't it? Folks that cheer you one day are ready to hang you the next."

"I am very aware of that, and I tread carefully. As for your future, Taza will talk to the council about this, but you are his prisoner, and he decides."

"I could make it easier for him."

"And how would you do that?"

"I could run, and he could decide I wasn't worth catching, and his problem would be gone."

Coyote Chaser nodded thoughtfully. "And Nitis would go with you."

"How'd you know that?"

"He has been asking too many questions about the white world lately. He keeps asking if it was hard for me in school being a half-breed, if the others made fun of me and were mean to me. I told him the truth. They were, and I eventually decided I would go to my mother's people who did not care. Fortunately, she saw to it that I learned the Apache language as well as English. That made me valuable as an interpreter for the People. Nitis would have such value in the years ahead, but during the age of his foolishness, he insists that he must see the white world for himself. He will likely return home someday."

"And maybe he's different. He's sure as the devil tougher than rawhide. Stubborn as a dang mule, too."

Coyote Chaser shrugged. "What you say is true. He will likely bring many surprises to all of us in the years ahead. I do not know what you plan, but I think it is best you tell me no more."

"Hell, I ain't got no plan. I'm waiting for some little kid to tell me what I do next."

"Whatever happens, I wish you well, my friend. You have been a very interesting guest of the Mescalero."

A week later at high noon, they approached an overflowing river. He assumed it must be the Rio Grande, and for the first time in months, Bushwa had a sense of where he might be located. Either Texas or New Mexico Territory should be on the other side of the river. The Mescalero would not want to be passing near larger settlements or soldiers of either army, so his guess was that they were some distance southeast of El Paso. Regardless, the river would once again become his guide if he kept it within sight and headed north.

They would hold up here for at least a night, maybe more, while scouts sought a crossing or until the river went down. With the possibility that Mexican soldiers were following, sooner would be better than later. It was unlikely that the army would cross the border in pursuit, and the officers would probably prefer to declare victory by claiming they had chased the invading Apache out of the country. Everybody would be happy.

The procession was hard to identify now, with stragglers several miles behind, and the main body spread out over the barren land like a grazing buffalo herd. Bushwa, mounted on Captain, tried to stay midway among the traveling horde, and he reined off to one side of the main body and dismounted. He was surprised when Nitis suddenly appeared at his side.

The boy got right to the point. "The council meets to-night. We should leave then, as soon as darkness comes."

"Not even wait for the verdict?"

"By then, it will be too late. Taza may take days to decide, or he may do so instantly. If he does not wait, and his decision is not favorable to you, it will be too late to escape."

"Yeah, I can see that. Do you know where we're at?"

"The Mexican town of Juarez is two days ride north along the river. The American town of El Paso is across the river. I have heard a ferry crosses the river between the two, but I do not know how the flooding affects that. I must leave the horse for my mother, so I will walk and run."

"Captain's a big critter, and he can carry us both off and on. I ain't much for walking, though. Seems like you got a lot of this figured out. It's against my nature to listen to a kid, but I'll give you the say-so for a spell."

"You take your horse as far to the north edge of the camp as you can without drawing too much attention. I will find you when darkness falls, and the council gathers. We will walk to the water's edge together, hoping most will think we are going to look at the river."

"With me leading my horse?"

"The People will be very tired and busy with eating. Some will be asleep already. We can only hope that none will raise an alarm. The night is on our side, and few would venture out into the darkness, especially to pursue an owl di-yin who has influence with the spirits. Even if your absence is noticed, I do not think they will come after us till morning. If scouts find a crossing, I question whether they will want to delay for a search with the possibility that Mexican soldiers are following. Certainly, not more than two or three warriors would be sent after us."

"What about your ma? Will she say anything about your missing?"

"I have told my mother. She does not like it, but she will know nothing and say nothing. I told her to tell my father that I will go where he instructed me when I can. She will learn where I am, and we will be reunited someday. I worry her constantly, so she is not too surprised. I go now. I will bring my bow and arrows and a blanket, maybe something to eat, but otherwise very little."

Nitis disappeared into the dust haze now being raised by the gathering of Apache who were carving out their family spaces. Things were happening a bit quickly even for Bushwa who was not generally inclined to give much thought to his actions. He still was saddened by the thought he would never see Nascha again. And then there was the child, whose life he would never be a part of. He was tempted again to give life as an Apache a longer try.

Still, it was Nascha who had divorced him the Apache way, and it would likely take months or years to convince Taza and Nascha that he was committed to the Mescalero. He could not fault them. He could not imagine lasting more than another month or two. He was no danged Apache and never would be.

That night, the first phase of Nitis's plan worked as the boy suggested. They had just strolled casually down to the river and walked away from the makeshift encampment, and there was no sign that anyone was curious. Bushwa was amazed at the boy's stamina as he trotted alongside Bushwa and his mount. They dared not push the horse any faster in the darkness because footing could be treacherous with the danger of possible stones or other unseen obstacles in their path. Besides, he wanted Captain rested in case warriors should give chase.

Several hours before sunrise, Bushwa spotted the spooky swaying of tree branches rising from the desert landscape and reined his gelding in that direction. Trees would often be a sign of water, maybe a bit of grass and something better to drink than that offered by the muddy Rio Grande. His hunch proved correct. He dismounted near a healthy cluster of desert willows surrounded by a ragged but ample carpet of assorted grasses, and, as he had suspected, a spring oozing up from a bed of small stones, pooling and then spilling over and soon disappearing into the surrounding sandy soil.

Bushwa said, "Let's fill our canteens and water jugs and then let Captain drink. I'll fetch our blankets, and we'll grab a few hours' shuteye. I'll stake out Captain so he can graze a bit and get some decent rest."

The sun was blinding when Bushwa emerged from his blanket cocoon. He had slept longer than intended. He sat up, groggy and yawning until he felt the cold steel of a rifle barrel pressed to his forehead. He looked up, "Morning, Taza. What you doing here?"

Taza said, "Get up."

Bushwa clambered to his feet and his eyes scanned the area for some sign of Nitis, and not seeing him, looked down at the boy's sleeping blanket and saw his head sticking above the blankets which had been anchored about him with a rawhide rope. His eyes were open wide in obvious fright, and a rag had been stuffed in his mouth to keep him quiet. Things were not looking so good right now.

Taza's sober face revealed nothing. "You leave Fox band?"

"Figured maybe I'd outworn my welcome."

"Not know what you say. Nascha say you go. She not go. Say not stop you."

"She wants you to let me go? Then why are you here?"

"Council say no. Want you to die."

"So you are here to kill me?"

"Taza is one to say."

"So what do you say?" Bushwa was buying time. His pistol rested in its holster beside the blanket. He had nothing to lose if he made a dive for it.

"Skunk hat."

"Skunk hat. What in blazes do you mean?"

"Want skunk hat."

Bushwa bent down and picked up the skunk hat that lay by his holstered gun, tempted for a moment to grab the gun before thinking better of it. He handed the hat to Taza, who placed it on his own head.

"Ban-jo."

"You want my banjo?" No, I can't let you have my banjo."

"Play when dead?"

He could not win this argument. His treasured banjo, protected in its leather case, rested in the stack of personal items where the hat had lain. He turned and bent over and picked it up, thinking again that the pistol was just inches away. Don't be a fool. Keep your head. He sighed and surrendered the instrument he loved.

"Get horse."

"My gray? No. I can't give up my horse." But he obeyed. As he walked fifty or so feet from their sleeping spot to collect Captain, he heard the distinctive pounding of a horse's hooves behind him. He turned. It was Taza riding his sorrel gelding and heading south, still wearing the skunk hat and the strap of the banjo bag wrapped over his neck and shoulder like an arrow sling, snugging Bushwa's treasure to his back. He realized in that moment he was going to live, but elation was subdued by the loss that rode away with a heathen who would not love it properly.

He walked back to Nitis, knelt, and pulled the silencing cloth from his mouth before removing the bonds that imprisoned him. He stood and extended a hand to the boy to help pull him to his feet.

Nitis, sounding out of breath, said, "I thought he was going to kill you and take me back to the People. And he brought the extra horse—one of Coyote Chaser's. I did not know he was here, and he had me tied before I woke and stuffed the rag in my mouth before I could warn you."

"Calm down, young feller. What extra horse?"

As though answering the question, a whinny came from the trees. "The brown mare with the white spots on her rump and backside. She was Coyote Chaser's favorite. She was to be a breeding mare. She is probably already with foal—it would be her first. After I was tied, Taza pointed to the mare before he led her into the trees."

Bushwa said, "He was telling you that the mare is yours. Coyote Chaser must have sent the horse. They must have talked before he left the Mescalero camp. And I'm betting that danged Coyote Chaser is going to teach hisself to play my banjo. He might even know how to pluck a few strings in the years he was raised in the white world. He's a cagey devil, that one."

"What do we do now?"

"Same as we started out to do. But I'd like to see what your ma sent along to eat first."

Chapter 37

June 1862

AFTER A WEEK at the Rough and Ready, Win was strong enough to walk from the bedroom to the outhouse, which gave him a revived sense of independence. The infection in the arrow wound had subsided noticeably, and he was confident today that healing was starting. Tomorrow, he hoped to be helping with chores, and he expected to be in the saddle again soon.

Renata had shifted into one of her quiet moods yesterday. He hoped she was not having second thoughts about their marriage. He assumed she was worried about Bodaway's delay in returning to report. She had expected him to be back no later than three nights ago. Win had reminded her that the Mescalero warrior had scouted for the Army many years and that he might be searching for other information that could be important in devising military strategy.

It was midmorning, and Win sat now on a bench off to one side of the station door, soaking in the warmth of a radiant sun that would turn fire-hot by afternoon. It was making him drowsy, though, and he was starting to nod off when he saw Renata walking toward him from the adjacent stable. She sat down beside him and leaned over and tendered a quick kiss on the cheek.

Renata said, "Are you ready to go back to work?"

"I'll do chores tomorrow for a start."

"I was teasing."

"I wasn't. I'm not good at doing nothing—never have been."

"I've noticed. We share that. Maybe we won't drive each other crazy."

"You're still going to marry me then?"

"Yes, of course. Unless you've changed your mind."

"Never. You'll never get rid of me. I want to get this done as soon as we get back across the river unless you are wanting a big, fancy wedding."

"No thank you. I had one of those, and it did not turn out well. Why would you think I might be having second thoughts?"

"You have been having a quiet spell. I'm never sure what's going on when you do that."

"I'm afraid you will have to get used to that. I do get lost in my thoughts. It would solve a lot of problems if we could get the Rebs out of Mesilla and Fort Fillmore. Besides marriage, aren't you wondering about what's next for us?"

"I don't much care as long as we're together."

"You're serious, aren't you?"

"Yep."

"You do love me, don't you?"

"Yep. A lot." He turned his head toward her. "Enough to give you a better kiss than the one I got a few minutes ago." He placed his hand behind her neck and pulled her to him, pressing his lips to hers with a deep, lingering kiss that triggered a response that said it was welcomed.

When he eased back, she said, "That was good, mister. I hope it won't be long and you can offer more."

"It won't be, I promise." Their kiss alerted him that the awareness of her next to him in bed was going to bring increasing temptation.

"A rider's coming," Renata said, pointing westerly. "Wrong direction for Bodaway."

"Moving at a slow pace, but I think it is Bodaway from the way he sits the horse."

As the rider drew closer, Renata said, "It is Bodaway." She got up to greet him, but Win was not ready to surrender his bench just yet.

Bodaway dismounted at the hitching rail and hitched his mount. Renata came up to him and gave the Apache a quick hug which he accepted stoically. "I have been worried about you."

"Ride much far. Many things to tell."

"Well, if I can get Win off his fanny, let's go inside and talk. Butch is baking bread, and I'm sure he's got coffee. He's chopping up the last of his ham today to put in gravy to pour over the bread, so there should be plenty for dinner this noon. Since you're here, he might even break out some beans if he's got any left." Bodaway loved coffee, and Win figured that was all the inducement he required.

Food supplies, even with the modest replenishment brought back from Mexican Springs, were drying up, and they desperately needed to get to Las Cruces or Mesilla to resupply. If nothing else, Martina, a hoarder of such things, would be able to help. Win figured he could make the trip to Las Cruces in a week's time if he could cross the river. He and Renata might try some hunting before then. With wagon traffic halted because of war or flooding, he wondered if the general stores had much left to sell.

He got up and followed Renata and Bodaway into the station, and soon they were all seated at the table, each with a mug of steaming coffee within easy reach. "Now," Renata said, "What did you learn?"

"Many things. Mesilla not west of river now."

"What? You mean it flooded out? It's gone?"

Win said, "I'm betting the river channel changed. When I last looked, the town had water on all sides. I wondered if that might happen. The Rio Grande cut a new channel. That means the Army will be forced to cross the river to retake the town and Fort Fillmore. Is that right, Bodaway?"

"Yes, right. River move, not town."

"Unbelievable," Renatta said. "This will be valuable information for the Union Army, but in a way, it creates a bigger problem."

"Go north with river to Fort Thorn. Army can cross river there. Two day's ride maybe."

Renata said, "You are worth pure gold, Bodaway. I will see that you get credit for this."

"Just want money. No pay long time. No more scout, no pay."

"I'm sorry. I will talk to the commanding officer when the Army comes. I hadn't thought of that. You probably haven't been paid since the Confederates took control of the territory."

"Two day, soldiers be here. I go to mountain. Look west. Many soldiers come. Horseback."

"That explains why you came from the west. You have been very busy."

"I eat and go home to People. Something not good happen there, I know."

Win said, "Bodaway, I have hesitated to ask, but I must. I have a friend who was taken captive by Mescalero, a stocky man with a banjo. Do you know of this man? I just want to know if he is still alive. I will not cause your people any trouble."

Bodaway was silent for a long time before he spoke. "We trade. Renata and Win, I know you marry. Son Nitis twelve summers old now want to live with whites, go school, learn white ways."

Renata looked at Win, and he nodded approval. Renatta said, "You bring your son to us. He will live with us in Las Cruces when the war is ended. Some schools are closed because of the war, but I was a teacher for two years at Fort Bliss. I can help him until schools are open again. You can visit. Perhaps times will change enough that he can go back and forth like you do."

"Nitis talk good white. Read words from book. Write."

"That's amazing. He will be welcome."

"Nitis do work, too. Know horses."

Win was getting impatient. "You mentioned a trade."

"Friend is in my band. Owl Man. Di-yin."

"Di-yin? What is that?"

"Man with powers to fight bad spirits. Friend fight owl spirits. Important to People. Owl Man marry chief's sister."

"That sounds like the Bushwa Sparks I always knew. The ornery devil always had a way of turning disaster into profit. Can he leave when he wants?"

"Must stay with Mescalero."

"Do you mean forever?"

"Till die or get away."

"So, he is still a prisoner?"

"Yes."

"He won't stay. If he doesn't talk his way out, your Owl Man will make a run for it when he figures the time is right."

Bodaway shrugged. "Nitis go with him."

"You think your son will leave with him?"

"I ask council to let me bring him with me. They say no. If Nitis run away, will find way to Rough and Ready. I tell him this."

Butch had been puttering in the kitchen area during the conversation, and Win figured the old station manager had not missed a word. Now he spoke. "If he ever shows up, Bodaway, I'll keep the youngster safe here till I get word to Ren."

Win doubted they would ever see the Mescalero boy or Bushwa, but maybe fate was at work with the bizarre coincidences that gave him hope that he might yet reunite with Bushwa.

Chapter 38

July 1862

C OLUMNS OF UNITED States Cavalry were lined up less than a mile distant from the Rough and Ready Station. Win and Renata stood outside the station as three riders separated from the main body and rode in their direction. As they neared, Renata recognized Sergeant Frank Hammer and the Navajo scout, Atsa Youngblood. The other rider, from his bearing and wide-brimmed hat, she assumed was an officer with some authority.

Having spent much of her childhood and early years of a marriage on Army posts, she had developed an instinct about such things. Several minutes later, as the men rode up and dismounted, Renata saw from his insignia that the officer was a lieutenant colonel.

Sergeant Hammer walked up to Win and Renata and offered a little bow. "Mister and Missus Evans, it's my pleasure to introduce Lieutenant Colonel Edward E. Eyre of the First California Volunteer Cavalry. He is commander of the mission and wanted to hear your report firsthand." She had almost forgotten that she and Win had passed themselves off as husband and wife at Mexican Springs.

The colonel was a tall, slender, fit-looking man, clean-shaven except for a thin, gray mustache. He had a grim set to his mouth that suggested he did not smile often. He doffed his hat, revealing a dense growth of graying hair. "Your service to the Union cause is much appreciated folks. I am anxious to hear your report."

"Come inside, gentlemen, and we will bring you up to date."

When they were seated at the table, Butch brought coffee, which she knew hurt him because the supply was nearly depleted. Renata said, "Win, why don't you give the update?" She knew she had surprised him, but to his credit, he took it in stride.

"You have seen the earlier reports, of course, but there is at least one major development. Mesilla now joins Fort Fillmore on the east side of the Rio Grande. The Rio Grande cut a new channel that put Mesilla on the other side of the river. As of a few days ago, the river was still out of its banks and virtually uncrossable. I don't think there is any way the water could have receded quickly enough to allow crossing."

Colonel Eyre opened a leather folder that he carried with him and pulled out several sheets of paper and a pencil and began to write. He obviously was a serious note taker. "Hmm. I hate to wait long. There is a practical matter of feeding troops and animals for any great length of time."

"The Mescalero scout that works with us said the river can be crossed at old Fort Thorn. I guess it is a few days north of Mesilla."

"I have a map showing the location of all Army forts and supply posts in this area. Fort Thorn has been abandoned but will be easy to locate. We will head north and cross there, then turn back south again and hit the Confederates if necessary. We have over five hundred soldiers. We will be dividing up with roughly half riding south to take Fort Bliss, but we will outnumber the Rebels at Fillmore and Mesilla, and odds are they will have retreated long before we arrive. The stars and stripes will soon replace the stars and bars over Fort Fillmore."

"Do you have any other questions, sir?"

"Our scouts have not seen signs of a good water supply here. We can travel for four or five hours yet. Is there water within that distance?"

Renata said, "No more than four hours. You can see the Organ Mountains to the north. They will come closer as you move east along the Butterfield Trail. You will pass through canyons along the way and several flooding streams. If you spread your troops out, you should find ample water in the canyons now. A month from now there likely won't be much more than a drop."

The colonel turned to Youngblood and said, "Atsa, why don't you and your scouts ride ahead and locate water sources?"

Renata said, "Atsa, I thought you were on your last mission at Mexico Springs."

He gave a small smile. "Money." He stood and headed out the door.

"That reminds me, Colonel. Our scout has not been paid for months. He will not help further without payment."

"I can understand that. I will send my quartermaster over. He is acting as paymaster for this mission. You can discuss this with him."

Win said, "One final matter, Colonel.

Eyre sighed. "Yes, Mister Evans?"

"Do you happen to have a chaplain with your contingent?"

The colonel furrowed his brow. "Yes, we have three of them as a matter of fact."

"Can they perform civilian marriage ceremonies and provide a certificate?"

"Yes, you would be surprised how often this arises."

"My wife and I would like to legalize our marriage. In this part of the country, a couple cannot always find a preacher, and you can understand how the war has made this a problem."

"Of course. Are you Catholic?"

Win looked at Renata.

"Methodist," she said.

"Captain Russell is an ordained protestant minister— Presbyterian, I think, but I suppose that would be close enough."

"That would be fine," Win said.

"We won't be here long."

"The sooner the better."

"I will send him over as soon as I return to the troops. I'll leave the sergeant here as a witness, and I assume your friend, Butch, can be the other."

An hour later, Win and Renata were married.

Chapter 39

NITIS WAS LIKE no twelve-year-old Bushwa had ever encountered. The boy's mind worked like he was twice his calendar age, constantly looking ahead and strategizing. Having the young Mescalero with him was like carrying a map in his saddlebags. Nitis apparently had an image of West Texas and New Mexico Territory imprinted in his head because he knew where everything was in this godforsaken country and the time it would take to reach any destination.

They had wasted no time departing after the visit by Taza. Bushwa had not wanted to risk the young chief changing his mind. The town of Juarez, which was in the Mexican state of Chihuahua, Nitis explained, was just across the river from El Paso, Texas. There would be many Americans there, some outlaws escaping American authorities.

They were several miles outside the town, which Bushwa thought was larger than most American towns he had visited. Of course, he guessed St. Louis and New Orleans had been his biggest stops. The landscape was starting to be dotted by tiny adobes on small tracts that included sheds and pens with goats and pigs, as well as an occasional cow. Most had a donkey or two in separate pens, and chickens running free. Goats were not so hard to feed, and he supposed donkeys could be put out to graze if they weren't fussy about their eating, but he wondered what in blazes they fed pigs.

Bushwa said, "We need to find a place to hide out till we figure out where to go from here."

Nitis pointed toward a crumbling adobe dwelling several hundred feet northwest of the trail. "No goats or other animals."

"You're thinking nobody lives there?"

Nitis shrugged. "Maybe—maybe not."

"Guess we can take a gander. Squat for a few days if nobody's claiming it. Wouldn't be the first time I done such."

When they investigated the adobe, they found it was clearly abandoned. apart from a collection of big rats that quickly surrendered the premises for the moment. The few windows were shattered and only half of a splintered door remained, likely battered open when thieves tried to see what they could salvage. A small rickety table and two chairs remained. A straw mattress in what appeared to be a bedroom of the two-room structure was nearly shredded, and Bushwa assumed it had been a home for rats.

The place would serve as a windbreak, and even though he could see blue sky through several cracks in the ceiling, Bushwa figured the roof would shed the worst of any rain. Most important, they would be well off the trail and could fort up some if need be.

"Well," Bushwa said, "this is home for now."

"I am hungry."

"Yep, we got to get some food. There's got to be a trading post up the way. I got me some money yet if they take American gold, but I don't speak no Mexican and won't know if them folks is trying to hornswoggle me. If I see somebody friendly-looking outside one of them adobes, maybe I'll see if they can help me."

"I speak some Spanish. We had Mexican women at the rancheria taken as slaves and wives, captured children adopted by the band, too. I do not speak it as fluently as English, but I could help. But there will be Mexicans who know some English because of the many visitors to border towns. Whites never want to learn other languages. Americans expect everybody to learn theirs."

"Well, I sure as hell ain't taking on a new language, but I can't take you with me. You look too Injun. That'll bring on questions."

"Buy two sombreros, one for each of us. You should also purchase sheers to cut my hair."

Bushwa cocked his head and studied the boy. "There you go, making good sense again. Your coloring fits and you're already dressed mostly like a Mexican except for them moccasins, and danged if you wouldn't look like a young greaser with a haircut and sombrero plopped on your head."

"I can pack my moccasins and go barefoot."

"Well, I'll just leave you in charge of our little palace here and go see what I can find. I'll get vittles to tide us over for a few days."

When Bushwa returned three hours later, he was wearing a sombrero and leading a burro carrying a full cargo wrapped in canvas and a dead chicken slung over the side. Nitis, grinning and wide-eyed, rushed out to meet him. Bushwa handed Nitis the burro's rope and said, "Tie this little critter next to that post by the house, and we'll unload him in a bit. His name is 'Pablo.'"

Bushwa unsaddled his horse, carried the saddle into the house and didn't know what to make of the new look. The clutter had disappeared, even the old mattress had been dragged off someplace. All that remained was the table and chairs on the hardpacked dirt-clay floor.

"By gum, you got this place looking like a dang palace, Nitis. You could hire out as some rich folks' maid."

"It is better, I guess. I know nothing about living in such a place."

"Let's water the horses and get them staked out. Slim pickings here, but there ain't been nothing else gnawing the grass down for a spell. That seemed a decent well we found out back, likely because the river's so close. I got an old bucket for hauling water, but they'll have to drink one at a time."

When they had tended to the horses, they commenced unloading the burro. Bushwa said, "I got everything from a Mexican woman who was out in the yard with what looked like a hunnert kids when I was going by. She talked some American words and with pointing and waving we got by good enough. I got all of this from her, including Pablo. They had three donkeys, and what with all them kids, I don't think they could afford to feed him. Anyhow, I got everything for the ten-dollar gold piece, and the woman acted like she had struck it rich. I think she'd have tossed in a kid or two if I'd asked."

"I must learn more about money."

"I got no doubt you'll learn and be the richest Mescalero in the country—maybe the richest man."

He untied the canvas cover and dropped it on the ground and some of the contents tumbled off. He bent over and snatched up the scrunched-up sombrero that had been at the top of the load and handed it to Nitis. "You are now a Mexican."

Nitis pulled the hat on. "A little big maybe," Bushwa said. "Mariana—that was her name—took it from one of the kids. I told her I needed one for my son. She come up with everything I asked about, some of it a little rundown maybe. I got an old pot for boiling water. We got lots of dried beans, so I thought we could cook them in the pot. We got us an old hen to roast. Do you know how to defeather the dang thing? I hate doing that."

"Never a chicken but prairie hens and other birds. I will do that, and I can find and whittle some roasting sticks."

"You're in charge of the chicken, boy, and I'll do some beans. She put some kind of bread-looking stuff in there, too. Tonight, we fill our bellies." He did not mention the half bottle of tequila the woman claimed she kept around for medicine that had been a part of the deal. With that passel of kids, she couldn't be blamed for taking a nip now and then.

He liked the buxom woman and hoped the husband did something besides provide stud service. As for the liquor, he knew it was probably some kind of Mexican rotgut, but he wasn't in a mood to be fussy about it.

Chapter 40

AFTER THREE DAYS, Bushwa and Nitis departed the adobe with some regret. The place had started to feel like home. Nobody had disturbed them at the house during their stay, and they had an opportunity to scout the fringes of Juarez and investigate the river's status. Between El Paso and Juarez, the Rio Grande was flowing within its banks now, but just barely. It would still be dangerous to cross. Besides, their destination was the Rough and Ready, which Nitis was certain would be on the west side of the river anyhow.

They decided to follow the river's course north and forego El Paso. They could survive for a spell on the supplies Mariana had sold him and supplement them with deer or rabbit or other creatures they might hunt along the way.

They departed early morning moving on a rim of high ground above the river. Bushwa reined in and pointed easterly across the river. "Look."

"Army fort?"

"That's Fort Bliss. Our volunteers passed by it on our way north. Stopped to resupply, but the stars and bars was flying above it then. Not now. That's the stars and stripes, the United States of America flag. The Yankees have retaken Fort Bliss. Things been happening since I been gone."

"I do not understand. I know your people have been at war. Indian tribes war, too. Sometimes, Mescalero even fight with Chiricahua, but peace comes quickly."

"Well, I ain't trying to explain it all. That's what the politicians do, and they don't likely understand it all themselves. I don't know how the dang war ends, but the Rebs ain't going to hold this part of the country. Don't take no general to figure that out. Never voted and never will. I just want to mind my own business and have everybody else look after their own affairs. Just leave old Bushwa alone, and I'll take care of myself."

Bushwa decided he must have confounded the boy enough because Nitis was silent for the next few hours. Their pace was steady but slow, and late afternoon they veered toward the hills that seemed to erupt from nowhere periodically in the middle of this desert land. Nitis caught sight of deer tracks that he said would lead to water, and as he predicted, they came upon a spring that spilled out enough water to feed a stream that led to the river.

Deer had kept most of the grass eaten down, but they set up camp over a hundred feet from the water source near a cluster of oak trees at the base of the hills. Nitis crept away from camp for a short spell and returned with a rabbit, so they risked a small fire to boil some beans and roast the rabbit. His deal with Mariana was looking better all the time.

As they sat by the fire enjoying their meal, Bushwa asked, "How far you reckon we are from this Rough and Ready place?"

"I am not certain, but I do not think it can be far. Have you ever seen the Butterfield Trail?"

"I crossed it once with the Reb army. It's wagon rutted and hard to miss. Goes right to Mesilla and Las Cruces and then heads south."

"Las Cruces should only be a two to three-hours' ride. The towns are divided by the river. Did you notice the river seems to be dropping as we move north?"

"Yep. Don't matter to us none. From what you said, we're headed away from the river."

"Yes. West."

"I just hope we'll be welcome at this Rough and Ready."

Chapter 41

W IN WAS NEARLY recovered from the Apache arrow wound. Some lingering soreness beneath his shoulder and down his ribs was worst when he rose in the mornings and worked itself out during the day. He rarely knew boredom, but he was getting acquainted the past few days. It was time to head back to Las Cruces. He and Renata had been making plans for their future together, and he was anxious to get on with them.

He was cleaning stalls in the stable again, figuring that the three critters lodged there were likely enjoying the tidiest lodging in all the territory. Suddenly, Molly the mule started her obnoxious braying. Visitors. Instinctively, before he peered out the doorway, he grabbed the Spencer propped against the wall. Apache were not likely visitors, but he was not taking any chances.

He stepped out and saw two riders, one leading a donkey, emerging from the dust and heading for the station. There was no urgency in their pace, and he relaxed. As the riders emerged from the veil of dust, he recognized the big rider astride his dapple gray: Bushwa Sparks, absent the trademark skunk cap and wearing a Mexican sombrero.

He raced from the stable to the front of the station and saw that Renata and Butch were each at a window, waiting to be certain the visitors posed no threat, likely with their own rifles ready. Win waved at Bushwa as he approached.

Bushwa waved back and hollered, "Win Evans. What in the hell are you doing here?"

When he reached the hitching rail, Bushwa dismounted, abandoned his horse and lumbered toward Win, grabbing him in a near-crushing bear hug, Win took a shot of pain to his injured flesh but just laughed. Bushwa released him and stepped back, surveying him with the missing-toothed grin spread across his bearded face.

"Welcome back, Bushwa. It's been well past the two months you promised, but I feared I would never see you again."

"I been a busy man, kid. Had me a good enough time but figured it was time to move on."

"You brought a friend with you." Win nodded toward the sober-faced Mexican boy who had not dismounted.

"Oh, this here is Nitis. He come with me from the Mescalero."

"He's not Bodaway's boy, by chance?"

"Do you know Bodaway?"

"Saved my life is all. Nitis, do you speak some English?"

"Yes, I speak English. I hope to improve, but we should not have a language problem."

Win was embarrassed to have asked the question. "Well, climb on down. We've got a lot to talk about."

Win felt Renata's hand on his shoulder. "Oh, Bushwa, I would like to have you meet my wife, Renata. Ren, this is the famous Bushwa Sparks, and the young man is Bodaway's son, Nitis."

Renata stepped forward and offered Bushwa her hand. "My pleasure, Bushwa. I've heard so much about you."

Bushwa took her hand, gave an exaggerated bow and kissed it. "I'm honored to make your acquaintance, ma'am." He straightened and looked at Win. "And how in blazes did you win over this beautiful princess? She'd have her pick of eligible bachelors and a fair number that wasn't."

Renata smiled and moved to the boy and welcomed him. Soon, they were engaged in serious conversation, and she had her arm wrapped about his shoulders. Nitis did not seem to mind.

Bushwa had not been changed by whatever he had experienced these past months. He was still worthy of his moniker. "Butch Zimmer is standing in the doorway. He's the station manager. Why don't you go on in? I'm betting he can still come up with coffee, and he was baking a cake this morning. You can get started with your lies while I put up your critters. I can stack the burro's load for you to sort through later and bring your saddlebags into the station."

Nitis said, "I will help, Mister Win."

Bushwa said, "Well, why don't you do that, Nitis? I can get rid of you for a spell

while I get to know this pretty lady."

That was Bushwa. He would never protest somebody else taking over a task. Win and Nitis led the animals into the stable. The boy seemed confused by the arrangement, so Win explained how the stall system worked while they unsaddled the horses and unpacked the burro. By the time they were finished with chores, Nitis was chattering like they were old friends. The boy's proficiency in the English language was mind-boggling and Win suspected that Nitis had an intelligence that should be carefully cultivated. This was no ordinary child in any race or culture.

When they went into the station, they found that Bushwa had made himself at home and was regaling a new audience with stories of his adventures. Win knew from experience that the tales would be embellished and revised with each retelling, but each new version became a new truth to his former employer.

Butch offered Nitis fresh water and pushed the plate of cookies in front of him, and the boy tasted one, grinned and nodded approvingly, and downed three. Later, Win noticed that the boy was tired and asked if he wanted to nap. The boy was agreeable, but when Win offered him the bed in the bedroom, he declined and asked to spread his blankets in the stable. Bushwa indicated that the stable would be paradise compared to recent lodging, so the decision as to where to sleep the newcomers was easily resolved.

Later that evening, after a good supper prepared by Butch and Renata, Win and Bushwa sat on the bench outside the station, enjoying a balmy breeze that was cooling the surrounding desert. They had serious matters to discuss, and Win knew that Renata had agreed to teach Nitis how to play checkers to give the two men private time.

Also, unsurprisingly, she had immediately taken to the boy, and they were on the way to becoming fast friends.

Bushwa said, "I can see you won't be moving on with me. That female has got you hogtied good."

"I like it in this country, Bushwa. It's different than any place I've ever lived, but I fit this land somehow, and Ren's got family here. I don't have such ties anyplace. Together, we'll do some serious ranching, horses and mules for now but cattle later. I've got my eye on ten thousand acres owned by Ren's aunt, if I can earn a little money and convince her to hold the land a bit longer. That way, I can bring something of my own to the marriage."

"What's land selling for in this country?"

"Dollar an acre would buy it."

"Make a deal for ten thousand dollars. Tell her you will pay a thousand down and that much each year plus interest on the balance for nine years. Give her a note and mortgage for the balance."

"You make it sound easy. I can't come close to the down payment, and Ren doesn't have any money either."

"You got your down payment. You still holding that gold coin of mine?"

"Yes, of course."

"There's over two thousand dollars there. Half is yours. You've earned it working for me these past years. We was more partners than boss and worker, and I didn't pay you half the time, did I?"

"Well, no, but I figured I was getting an education, and you kept me boarded and fed."

"I always intended to make it right with you when we parted ways. That time is now."

"I don't know what to say. I can't thank you enough."

"You got to see to Nitis good, though. See that he gets the best schooling a kid can get. He's scary smart, but I feel connected to him somehow."

"We'll look after Nitis. You don't have to worry about that. But Bodaway said you had a wife."

"Her name is Nascha. Like all the other females I've tied the knot with, she done divorced me, then went and disappeared. And I'm going a long, long way from here."

Win could tell Bushwa did not want to talk about the woman, but there was a hurt in Bushwa's tone that made him think that Nascha had meant something to his friend. "If you stay close by, maybe a time would come that you could find her and patch things up."

"I ain't cut out to be no Apache, and some things you just got to ride away from and put behind you. I'm heading to someplace that's got trees and green grass. I've heard stories about Wyoming Territory. Nitis says I just go straight north, pass through Santa Fe and Denver,

Colorado along the way. Might take me a year or so, but I'm thinking I'll try that out unless I run into something that suits me along the way."

"You've already decided, haven't you?"

"Yep."

Chapter 42

BUSHWA WANTED TO ride north from the Rough and Ready, but he needed his money, so he accompanied Win, Renata and Nitis to the Rutledge Boarding House. A ferry was available to cross the Rio Grande's new channel to Mesilla and the water level in the river was dropping daily. It appeared that water would be no hinderance on his next journey. He decided to let the Rio Grande be his guide for as far as it would lead him to places that made sense.

He stayed two nights at the Rutledge boarding house as their guest. It pleased him to see Nitis settled in a room, although he could see the boy preferred the floor to a bed for now. He would get over that soon enough.

He took a liking to Martina Rutledge who spoiled him rotten for two days. If she had been a single lady, he thought he would have stayed around longer to see what might happen between them.

The second evening, he and Win sat at the dining table after the others had retired and made the money split. Win still was uneasy about it, but Bushwa pointed out that he would have plenty of money for a fresh start in Wyoming and that he would likely triple it along the way. "Call it a wedding gift if you want, but I wouldn't sleep nights if I left with your share of the money." Of course, he was lying, he didn't lose sleep over such things. The only thing that cost him sleep was thinking about Nascha and the little one that was sprouting from the seed he had planted.

That night with gold coins stacked on the table, Bushwa counted out a separate stack of double eagles. "There is five hundred dollars there. I want you to keep that for Nascha. I never told you that she is with child. Someday, you'll know when the time is right—it might be years—I want you to see that she gets this, or if she's not around that the child does. Nitis can help make this happen."

He did not like good-byes. The next morning, well before sunrise, he saddled Captain. He led the horse from the stable and stepped into the saddle. He looked up at the starlit sky and picked out the North Star. It was time to follow it to Wyoming Territory.

Author's Note

The Civil War battles between North and South over the western states and territories tend to be a mere footnote in most histories of the war. The captures of Fort Fillmore and Fort Bliss and the hard-fought victory at the Battle of Valverde gave the Confederacy hope for the conquest of the vast lands.

Bushwa is set in 1862, the year that the South's vision of dominion over the West collapsed. The Rebels took Santa Fe briefly but failed to overcome nearby Fort Union. Finally, in the spring, Confederate troops were defeated soundly at Glorieta Pass in the Sangre de Cristo mountains in northern New Mexico, and supplies depleted, the Rebel army commenced a chaotic retreat to San Antonio. Like dominoes, Fort Fillmore, Fort Bliss, and other sites fell to the Union with little resistance.

By the time Bushwa Sparks departed Las Cruces for Wyoming Territory, the war in the West had effectively ended.

The author also wishes to acknowledge that a vital resource for this novel has been a non-fiction work by James L. Haley, "APACHES, A history and Culture Portrait" (1981)."

About the Author

Ron Schwab is the author of the popular Western series, The Blood Hounds, Lockwood, The Law Wranglers, The Coyote Saga, and The Lockes. His novels Grit and Old Dogs were both awarded the Western Fictioneers Peacemaker Award for Best Western Novel, and Cut Nose was a finalist for the Western Writers of America Best Western Historical Novel.

Ron and his wife, Bev, divide their time between their home in Fairbury, Nebraska and their cabin in the Kansas Flint Hills.

For more information about Ron Schwab and his books, you may visit the author's website at www.RonSchwabBooks.com.